W9-AHA-541

Captain's Log

July 10

Today we took on a distraction the size of the Titanic-sinking iceberg. She might look great in a pair of shorts, but her presence is already disrupting the crew, turning a bunch of practical, hardworking men into giddy schoolboys. There's no room on this ship for a good-looking, starry-eyed dreamer. Kayla Waterton has to go!

It shouldn't be hard to convince her to leave. She says she wants to be one of the crew— so I'll put her to work. A few midnight survey shifts, and she'll be begging to go back to the comfortable world she knows. My own sanity depends on it!

A Tale of the Sea

MORE THAN MEETS THE EYE by *Carla Cassidy*
IN DEEP WATERS by *Melissa McClone*
CAUGHT BY SURPRISE by *Sandra Paul*
FOR THE TAKING by *Lilian Darcy*

Dear Reader,

There's no better escape than a fun, heartwarming love story from Silhouette Romance. So this August, be sure to treat yourself to all six books in our sexy, sizzling collection guaranteed to keep you glued to your beach chair.

Dive right into our fantasy-filled A TALE OF THE SEA adventure with Melissa McClone's *In Deep Waters* (SR#1608). In the second installment in the series about lost royal siblings from a magical kingdom, Kayla Waterton searches for a sunken ship, and discovers real treasure in the form of dark, seductive, modern-day pirate Captain Ben Mendoza.

Speaking of dark and seductive, Carol Grace's *Falling for the Sheik* (SR#1607) features the mesmerizing but demanding Sheik Rahman Harun, who is nursed back to health with TLC from his beautiful American nurse, Amanda Reston. Another royal has a heart-wrenching choice to make in *The Princess Has Amnesia!* (SR#1606) by award-winning author Patricia Thayer. She survived a jet crash in the mountains, but when the amnesia-stricken princess remembers her true social standing, will she— can she—forget her handsome rescuer...?

Myrna Mackenzie's *Bought by the Billionaire* (SR#1610) is a Pygmalian story starring Ethan Bennington, who has only three weeks to transform commoner Maggie Todd into a lady. While Cole Sullivan, the hunky, all-American hero in Wendy Warren's *The Oldest Virgin in Oakdale* (SR#1609), is coerced into teaching shy Eleanor Lippert how to seduce any man—himself included.

Then laugh a hundred laughs with Carolyn Greene's *First You Kiss 100 Men...* (SR#1611), a hilarious and highly sensual read about a journalist assigned to kiss 100 men. But there's only one man she *wants* to kiss....

Happy reading—and please keep in touch!

Mary-Theresa Hussey

Mary-Theresa Hussey
Senior Editor

Please address questions and book requests to:
Silhouette Reader Service
U.S.: 3010 Walden Ave., P.O. Box 1325, Buffalo, NY 14269
Canadian: P.O. Box 609, Fort Erie, Ont. L2A 5X3

In Deep Waters

MELISSA McCLONE

SILHOUETTE *Romance*®

Published by Silhouette Books

America's Publisher of Contemporary Romance

If you purchased this book without a cover you should be aware that this book is stolen property. It was reported as "unsold and destroyed" to the publisher, and neither the author nor the publisher has received any payment for this "stripped book."

Special thanks and acknowledgment are given to
Melissa McClone for her contribution to
A TALE OF THE SEA series.

For Mackenna and Finn

SILHOUETTE BOOKS

ISBN 0-373-19608-3

IN DEEP WATERS

Copyright © 2002 by Harlequin Books S.A.

All rights reserved. Except for use in any review, the reproduction or utilization of this work in whole or in part in any form by any electronic, mechanical or other means, now known or hereafter invented, including xerography, photocopying and recording, or in any information storage or retrieval system, is forbidden without the written permission of the editorial office, Silhouette Books, 300 East 42nd Street, New York, NY 10017 U.S.A.

All characters in this book have no existence outside the imagination of the author and have no relation whatsoever to anyone bearing the same name or names. They are not even distantly inspired by any individual known or unknown to the author, and all incidents are pure invention.

This edition published by arrangement with Harlequin Books S.A.

® and TM are trademarks of Harlequin Books S.A., used under license. Trademarks indicated with ® are registered in the United States Patent and Trademark Office, the Canadian Trade Marks Office and in other countries.

Visit Silhouette at www.eHarlequin.com

Printed in U.S.A.

Books by Melissa McClone

Silhouette Romance

If the Ring Fits... #1431
The Wedding Lullaby #1485
His Band of Gold #1537
In Deep Waters #1608

Yours Truly

Fiancé for the Night

MELISSA McCLONE

has a degree in mechanical engineering from Stanford University, and the last thing she ever thought she would be doing is writing romance novels, but analyzing engines for a major U.S. airline just couldn't compete with her "happily-ever-afters."

When she isn't writing, caring for her two young children or doing laundry, Melissa loves to curl up on the couch with a cup of tea, her cats and a good book. She is also a big fan of *The X-Files,* and enjoys watching home decorating shows to get ideas for her house—a 1939 cottage that is *slowly* being renovated.

Melissa lives in Lake Oswego, Oregon, with her own real-life hero husband, daughter, son, two lovable but oh-so-spoiled indoor cats and a no-longer-stray outdoor kitty who decided to call the garage home. Melissa loves to hear from readers. You can write to her at P.O. Box 63, Lake Oswego, OR 97034.

A TALE OF THE SEA

Family Tree

King Okeana (d.) m. Queen Wailele (d.)

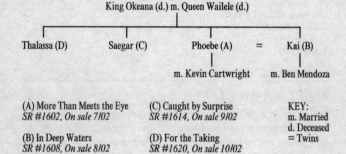

Thalassa (D) Saegar (C) Phoebe (A) = Kai (B)

m. Kevin Cartwright m. Ben Mendoza

(A) More Than Meets the Eye
SR #1602, On sale 7/02

(B) In Deep Waters
SR #1608, On sale 8/02

(C) Caught by Surprise
SR #1614, On sale 9/02

(D) For the Taking
SR #1620, On sale 10/02

KEY:
m. Married
d. Deceased
= Twins

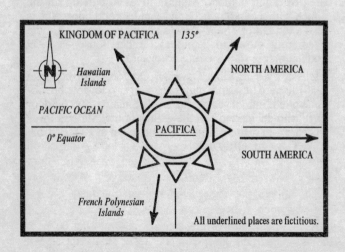

Prologue

"Please tell me about Atlantis, Daddy."

Jason Waterton covered nine-year-old Kayla with a quilt and tucked in the edges. "What about the leprechauns?"

"Tomorrow. I want to hear about Atlantis tonight."

Her eyes, the same gray-green of her mother's, sparkled like the ocean at sunrise. Each year, Kayla's resemblance to her mother grew. Same eyes, same smile, same golden mane of hair. A heavy weight bore down on him, reminding him of all they'd left behind. How he missed—

"It's my favorite, but Heidi Baxter said Atlantis and mermaids don't exist." Lines formed on Kayla's forehead. "They're real, aren't they, Daddy?"

The hopeful tone in her voice tugged at Jason's heart. She was such a dreamer. A dreamer with a pure heart. Her classmates sometimes teased her about her belief in the whimsical, but he hoped she never changed. "If you believe they're real, they will be, love."

With a satisfied smile on her face, she snuggled against her pillow. "I believe."

"You must always believe." Jason kissed her forehead. The intensity of his love for her never ceased to amaze him. He couldn't imagine life without Kayla.

"I will." She smiled. "Can I hear about Atlantis now?"

He always gave her what she wanted. He only wished he could give her more. Jason sat on the edge of her twin bed. "A long time ago in a sea far, far away, a magical island called Atlantis existed. The people of Atlantis knew no hardship. The land provided unlimited food and natural resources. Science rid society of all diseases and invented technology to simplify life. It was a perfect existence.

"Until one day, smoke and ash spewed from a mountain in the center of the island. Lava flowed. The smell of sulfur made it difficult to breathe. The island fought bravely against the pressure of the volcano and the movement of the earth, but in the end lost the battle. Atlantis sank to the bottom of the ocean."

Kayla shivered. "That must have been so scary."

Jason held her small hand. "But Atlantis had been good to the sea, taking only what it needed and never any more. So the sea allowed a large dome of earth to cover the island and provide a pocket of air for the people to breathe. Scientists helped the people adapt to their new underwater home."

"The people became mermaids."

He nodded. "Over time, the people of Atlantis evolved into 'mer.' They could live in the sea with gills and a tail, or out of the sea with lungs and legs, but most preferred the freedom of the water." Jason closed his eyes for a moment. "To leave the confines of Atlantis behind... To be connected to the other creatures of the sea... To be surrounded by water and able to swim anywhere was...total exhilaration.''

Kayla sighed. "I wish I could be a mermaid."

"So do I, love—" Jason kissed her cheek "—so do I."

Chapter One

Foamy green swells tossed the supply ship back and forth like a child's plaything. Kayla Waterton grasped the railing and peered over the edge. She'd done her research and knew what to expect while at sea. Still, she couldn't hide her awe at the water's power or the secrets buried in the murky depths.

"This will keep you safe while you transfer to the other ship, Miss Waterton." Pappy, who looked more like Santa Claus than the ship's captain, connected a lifeline to her life jacket in case she fell into the water when she transferred to the other ship tied alongside them. "Just wish I knew what turned the water so rough all of a sudden."

As soon as the *Xmarks Explorer,* a survey-and-salvage ship, had appeared on the horizon, the calm waters had turned choppy. None of the supply ship's crew could explain why, but Kayla thought she knew the answer.

The sea was angry.

She wasn't supposed to be in the middle of the Pacific

Ocean. She'd promised her father she would stay away from the sea. If only he was here with her. But he was gone and she'd taken up where he'd left off—locating lost shipwrecks. Piecing together and solving the secrets of the past gave her such satisfaction. She found comfort reading old journals and maps, comparing cargo ledgers and insurance claims, putting the bits and pieces of research into reports for search expeditions.

And for the first time ever, she was going on an expedition herself. She couldn't deny her excitement, even though she'd had no choice in coming. Her father's dream had been to find the *Isabella*—a pirate ship of untold value lost nearly three centuries ago, but the bozo running the search expedition was looking in the wrong place, wasting valuable time and money.

"Are you ready, Miss Waterton?" Pappy asked.

Kayla nodded, but she felt less than confident. Spray from the swells hitting the ships flew through the air. She would have to walk right through the mist, but she was more worried about the waves washing over the narrow plank bridging the gap between the two ships. A shiver ran down her spine. Kayla liked reading about adventure on the high seas, not experiencing one herself.

Think about finding the Isabella, *locating the lost treasure, making Daddy's dream come true, finding the answers I need...* It was only water. So what if she got wet? She could do this. She *had* to do this.

"We'll bring your gear over with the supplies."

The sooner she got to the other ship, the sooner her search for the *Isabella* began. Kayla smiled. "Thank you, Pappy."

"Hold on and keep moving." He assisted her onto the gangway. "It's not that choppy, but whatever you do, don't look down."

She gripped the handrails and took a step. The plank moved up and down, following the motion of the waves. Water seeped through her shoes, wetting her socks and feet.

Don't look down.

That hadn't been in any of her books, but she knew good advice when she heard it.

Kayla stared at the crew standing on deck. She focused her gaze on one man with hair the color of coal. He stood out from the others. Though he was simply standing, he exuded a confidence and an arrogance Kayla found both appealing and unnerving.

With a gold hoop in his left ear, he was more pirate than white knight. It was much too easy to imagine him at the helm of the *Isabella,* barking orders to his crew, stealing treasures from ships sailing the Pacific and kidnapping their female passengers. No doubt he whispered seductive phrases in Spanish, if Kayla guessed his ancestry correctly, before ravishing the maidens locked in his cabin.

As if reading her mind, his dark-as-midnight eyes met hers with such intensity she almost took a step back.

She swallowed hard. Twice. It didn't help.

Dangerous was the only way to describe him. She wouldn't call him handsome. Not unless you liked tall-dark-ruggedly-sexy-one-hundred-percent-males. She didn't, but her body forgot that fact. For some strange reason, her pulse picked up speed. Adrenaline? Attraction? Standing midway across the plank, she wasn't sure of the difference right now.

The only thing she knew to do was keep moving.

Instinct told her to turn around, but she didn't. Instead, Kayla forced herself to walk toward him. Not him, the ship. She took another step and another. Moving closer,

Kayla found herself entranced, almost mesmerized, by his eyes.

Look away, look anywhere but at him.

She looked down. Right at the churning water. Oh, my…

"Watch out."

The warning registered, but it was too late. The wave smashed into her and tossed Kayla against the rail. She hit hard against her left hip. Cold water drenched her, soaked through her clothes. Saltwater stung her eyes and filled her mouth. Despite the slippery rail, she hung on. Lifeline or not, she wasn't taking any chances. She had researched what getting lost and rescued at sea entailed.

Strong arms lifted her and carried her onto the ship. She blinked to clear her eyes and came face-to-face with the pirate. His eyes were even darker up close. She shivered. From the cold.

"What were you doing just standing there?" Frustration—perhaps a little irritation—filled his voice. An all-American voice. No sexy foreign accent for this pirate, she realized with a twinge of disappointment. He drew his full lips into a thin line. "Do you always walk around with your head in the clouds?"

His comment brought back painful memories of being teased. She had never fit in at school. Or anywhere else. "I didn't do it on purpose."

"The least you could do is thank me for saving your life."

She didn't like his attitude, and she didn't like being held in his arms. Her legs felt prickly. "I didn't ask to be rescued."

As he released her from his arms, he laughed. Her legs quivered on the rocking deck and wouldn't support her weight. Kayla fell backward, landing with a not-so-graceful thump.

"You okay?" The tone of the pirate's voice softened. He sounded genuine.

Not trusting her voice, she nodded. Talk about a memorable entrance. She remained seated on the wave-tossed deck and he helped her out of her life jacket. He handed her a blanket. "Here."

She muttered thanks and dried herself. The world closed in on her, and she struggled to catch her breath. Kayla glanced up. Half a dozen men surrounded her. Not your average tenured history or archeology professor types, either. No, these guys would look more comfortable on the back of a Harley than in a classroom.

"Give the lady some room, boys," the pirate said. "You're crowding her."

The men backed away, and Kayla's breathing returned to normal. Perhaps the pirate wasn't so dark and dangerous, after all. Perhaps he was a prince in disguise. Perhaps a gentle heart lay beneath his rough exterior....

Her legs prickled again. "I'm sorry for any inconvenience."

"A little late for that." His face darkened into a scowl.

Okay, he wasn't a prince. She wasn't a princess, so they were even. But he stood way up there, and she sat way down here. Time to lessen his height advantage. She rose and managed not to fall again despite the pin-and-needle numbness in her legs. The blanket pooled at her wet sneakers. She ignored it.

Kayla would spend the next month or two with these people—make that men. She didn't want to start out on the wrong foot. She was a calm and cool professional.

She could handle this. "Thank you for getting me on board."

His frank appraisal made her blush. His mouth twisted. "I'm Ben Mendoza. This is my ship, my crew and my expedition."

So he was the one in charge and looking for the *Isabella* in all the wrong places. *Figures.* All looks, no brain. At least she wasn't itchy or shivering any longer. "I'm Kayla Water—"

"Look, Watertown—"

"It's Waterton," she corrected. "I realize your first impression of me might not be—"

"Why should my impression of you matter?"

She wet her lips. "Because we'll be working together."

He blew out a puff of air. "Now, that's a good one."

"I was sent here to help."

Ben frowned. "The museum sent you to legitimize the operation and appease the investors."

He had it all wrong. "But I'm—"

"Already a distraction."

Kayla didn't know what she'd done to upset him so much, but the expedition had bigger problems than searching in the wrong location. The pirate didn't want her here. Too bad. She had the right to be here, and she was staying. Somehow she would make this work. "Mr. Mendoza, there seems to be a misunderstanding."

"I understand things better than you think." His eyes narrowed. "And I have one simple rule for you to understand. Stay out of our way. We have *real* work to do, Mrs. Waterson."

A slap across the face would have hurt less, but she wasn't going to let him get to her. "It's Waterton. Ms., not Mrs."

"Today's our lucky day, boys," a grizzly voice said from behind her. One of the "boys," no doubt. "She's…single."

"When has that ever stopped you, Wolf?" a man with a distinctive Southern drawl asked.

The comments didn't seem to register with Ben. "Let's get one thing straight. I don't care if your name is H2O. No one wants you here but the investors and the museum."

"I wouldn't go that far, boss," the grizzly voice added.

Ben rolled his eyes. "But as long as you're here, you are my responsibility, so don't do anything stupid."

The "again" was implied. Kayla's mouth nearly gaped. He didn't have a clue as to why she was here or who she was. Damn Mr. Andrews, the museum's PR person, for not telling Ben more about her participation in the search. She imagined what his reaction would be when he learned the truth.

"Lucky me," she murmured.

Ben frowned. "Go change."

"I beg your pardon?"

He rolled his eyes again. This time it was directed at her. She didn't like that any better than she liked him.

"Common sense not part of your ivory-tower curriculum?"

Her cheeks burned, but she stared him straight in the eyes. "I blew that class off the same day I skipped the course you taught on rudeness."

He met her gaze but said nothing.

The seconds turned into a minute.

Damn Ben Mendoza. It wasn't supposed to be like this. How was she going to work with him? Kayla could barely breathe, and she couldn't blame it on claustrophobia. Her heart rate increased, and she felt warm. Hot, actually.

Much to her relief, he broke the silence first. "Lock the door to your cabin. My crew is all too human and you've already given us a sneak preview of your...wares."

Kayla glanced at her clothes plastered to her like a second skin. Great, she was a poster girl for a wet T-shirt contest. She crossed her arms over her chest and noticed the men with leering grins and glints in their eyes. "All too human" was putting it nicely. For a highly trained technical crew of shipwreck location specialists, they were a motley bunch. Add a Jolly Roger flag to the mast, and she would be on a pirate ship.

Ben stood in front of the door to Kayla Waterton's cabin. Twice he'd raised his hand to knock. Twice he hadn't.

He'd given her plenty of time to dry off, change clothes and unpack. He'd used the time to chill himself. He wasn't proud of his behavior on deck, but he'd been caught off guard.

Kayla Waterton wasn't what Ben had expected. That bothered him. Annoyed him. Frustrated him, too.

And he'd taken it out on her.

Real smart, Mendoza.

Some pro he'd turned out to be. But he couldn't help himself.

It was bad enough the museum had to send anyone out here in the first place. A knife in the back. Xmarks Explorers had been good enough to partner with when no one else wanted to chase down the legendary lost pirate ship. But now, after he'd made all the preparations and done all the work, they wanted to toss a ringer into the act. And not any ringer, a total looker who belonged on a catwalk and made men lose sight of what was important—their goals.

Ben Mendoza, meet your worst nightmare—Kayla Waterton.

Bulky life jacket aside, she'd stood on the gangplank looking more like a sea nymph than a maritime historian. By definition, a historian should have her hair pulled back into a tight bun, her body disguised by shapeless, gray, nonfeminine clothing and her eyes hidden behind a pair of bottle-thick glasses. He could have lived with that sort of woman on his ship. His crew, too. She would have been a pain, but she wouldn't have been a distraction.

Unlike Kayla. She was a distraction the size of the *Titanic*-sinking iceberg, and twice as dangerous.

Her long blond hair shimmered even with the overcast skies. Hair like hers was supposed to be worn loose—brushing the middle of her back or a man's chest. Contorting her hair into a tight bun would constitute a criminal act.

And those eyes…an intriguing blend of green and gray, a mixture of colors from the sea and sky. Staring into her eyes, he'd felt a moment of recognition, a sense of déjà vu. A familiar gnawing in his gut made him realize why. Kayla had a dreamy quality in her eyes. Similar to his father and his ex-wife.

The appreciative sighs and catcalls from his crew had echoed the jolt of attraction shooting through Ben the nanosecond he saw her.

But Ben had no room in his life for another good-looking, starry-eyed dreamer to mess up his hard work and his plans. He had a ship to find. He wasn't about to fail—he couldn't afford to. The crew and Madison were counting on him to deliver. He wasn't going to blow this. Or let anyone else blow it for him.

Kayla Waterton had to go.

The investors and the Museum of Maritime History wanted her here. They were co-sponsors of the expedition and held the purse strings, so he wouldn't go against their wishes. But now that she'd arrived, all Ben had to do was make her decide to leave.

An idea formed. A bit devious, but she was the one who didn't belong here. She was the one who was going to get in their way.

Life on a salvage ship might be adventurous, romantic to some. But the reality was a far cry from images of opening a chest full of gold and jewels. A middle-of-the-night survey assignment, and Kayla would be begging to go back to the comfortable confines of her ivory-tower world.

Ben smiled. He'd make her feel like one of the crew, put her to work and watch disillusionment take over. The sooner she left his ship, the sooner he and the crew could concentrate on finding the *Izzy*.

He knocked. The lock bolt clicked after a few seconds and the door opened. At least she followed instructions.

Kayla stared at him. Silence stretched between them like the calm before the storm.

"Do you need anything?" he asked finally.

"No."

She wasn't going to make this easy for him. Okay. He deserved it. "About what happened earlier…"

She'd changed into a pair of well-worn jeans and a white shirt. Damn, she looked good. Almost as good dry as she had wet.

He leaned against the doorjamb. "I was—"

"A jerk."

He shifted his weight. "That's one way to put it."

"A tyrant."

"That's another." Apologizing wasn't his strong suit. Nor was idle chitchat. But he deserved this, too. "I...I'm..."

He thought about the *Izzy*. Some had called the search for the ship a pipe dream, since many believed she didn't exist. At first Ben had seen the search as nothing more than a job. But after two seasons of looking for the *Izzy*, the search had become more. He wasn't about to lose funding.

No matter how he felt about Kayla Waterton, Ben couldn't let ego or pride get in the way now. Not when he was so close to finding the lost pirate ship and her stolen treasures he could taste it. Finding the *Izzy* would change his life, his crew's lives and, most important, his daughter's life. He wouldn't fail.

"I'm sorry," he said.

Kayla's brows furrowed, wrinkling her forehead. Something told Ben not to rush her. He stood and waited.

"Apology accepted." The pink tip of her tongue darted out and wet her lower lip. "Did you want anything else?"

Besides you. The random thought hit too close to home. He hadn't wanted anything else—anything but the *Izzy*—until Kayla arrived. He would have to keep his distance. Not the easiest thing to do on a ship this size, but the last thing he wanted were any personal complications that could jeopardize the expedition. "A second chance."

Her gaze met his, and Ben's temperature shot up ten degrees. The heat seemed to be generating between them.

She extended her hand. "Kayla Waterton."

"Ben Mendoza." He took her hand in his. Her skin was soft and smooth and tanned. She might spend time outdoors, but he expected the only manual labor she did was carrying books from the library. "Welcome aboard the *Xmarks Explorer*."

"Daddy, Daddy." Madison, his three-year-old daughter, barreled into him. She carried her favorite doll and constant companion, Baby Fifi. "I'm done sleeping."

"You're not supposed to leave your cabin by yourself."

"But I'm done sleeping and I heard footsteps." She grinned, and Ben smiled. Madison had him wrapped around each of her little fingers and toes. "Is this her?"

Ben stared at his daughter. Forty-odd inches of sugar, sunshine and smiles. She wasn't a perfect child, but he wasn't a perfect father. Together they made a pretty good pair. Loving warmth settled around his heart, as soft and comforting as Madison's baby blanket.

"Kayla, this is my daughter, Madison." He stepped out of the doorway. "Madison, this is Miss Waterton."

Kayla kneeled down to Madison's level and shook her hand. Both had long hair, but his daughter's was as dark as Kayla's was light. "Madison Mendoza. What beautiful alliteration."

Madison scrunched her brows. "Alli—what?"

Kayla smiled. "You have a pretty name."

"Thank you."

"How old are you?"

Madison raised three fingers. "Three." She tugged on his arm. "When does the other lady come, Daddy?"

"What other lady, princess?"

"Peyna Deass."

Ben scratched his head. Madison was a chatterbox,

but he still had trouble deciphering some of her phrases. Before he could ask her again, she slipped inside Kayla's cabin and fiddled with a cabinet latch. "Madison, this isn't your cabin."

"It's okay," Kayla said to his surprise. "She can't hurt anything."

"You'd be surprised what those little fingers can get into." He peered around Kayla. Madison played with the latch, oblivious to everything else. She was growing up so fast. Too fast. She was the main reason he wasn't about to screw up finding the *Izzy*. He wouldn't let her down.

"Figure out who she's talking about yet?" Kayla asked.

"No," Ben admitted. Ladies never came aboard the ship. Until Kayla.

"She's talking about me."

"But you're not—"

"A pain in the ass?" Kayla whispered.

Oh, hell. He was going to have to watch his language around Madison. Normally he was better, but every so often he forgot she was three years old. He'd have to have a little talk with Madison. And one with himself, too. "Kids…"

Kayla's eyes sparkled with laughter. So the pretty historian had a sense of humor. Why wasn't he more relieved?

"Daddy?" Madison glanced up, her eyes wide with excitement. "When does Peyna Deass arrive? I want to roll in the hay with her." She turned to Kayla. "Daddy says that's what she needs to do."

"On that note, I'd better put my little magpie back in her cage."

"I want to see the little magpie, Daddy. Is it in your

room?'' Before he could say a word, Madison skipped down the passageway toward his cabin.

''She's cute.''

''Sometimes a little too cute,'' he admitted. ''What she said—''

''Why don't we make your original apology all-inclusive?''

He couldn't believe she was letting him off so easily. ''Deal.''

''Speaking of which, do you want to start over again?'' A smile as wide as the Panama Canal lit up Kayla's face, and Ben's breath caught in his throat. She introduced herself and winked. ''Third time's the charm.''

Okay, she had a great smile and a sense of humor. Not to mention a great body and face. Not that he was interested, but it didn't hurt to look.

''So are you going to be the lucky charm that leads us to the *Izzy?*''

Kayla nodded. ''Most definitely.''

Over his dead body. ''You sound confident.''

''I am,'' she admitted. ''Because I know where the *Isabella* is…and you don't.''

Chapter Two

She shouldn't have said that.

It may have been the truth, but the moment the words escaped, Kayla regretted them. She'd glimpsed a softer side of Ben during his interaction with Madison. A side Kayla liked. She didn't want to antagonize him and bring the mean pirate back.

Too late.

His eyes darkened; his nostrils flared. If he could breathe fire, she would be toast.

And then he laughed.

Kayla did a double take.

Yes, Ben Mendoza was definitely laughing. The deep, rich sound rippled through the air and surrounded her. His laugh was warm and intriguing and much too appealing. She didn't know whether to be relieved or worried.

"That's a good one." The crinkles at the corners of his eyes should have made him look older. Harder. Instead, they took years off and softened the rugged planes of his face. Kayla's heart beat triple-time. "You had me going for about thirty seconds."

He didn't believe her. Worse, he was laughing at her. Kayla's blood boiled. She dug her nails into her palms.

What nerve. She'd felt guilty for saying something that might upset him when he was still a total jerk. And here she thought he was a sensitive father.

The man was as soft as an abalone. A mixture of embarrassment and anger washed over her. She wanted to tell him what she thought of his expedition. She wanted to tell him why he'd better listen to her.

She wanted to tell him where he could stick it.

Be poised, confident. You are the one in charge. Kayla tilted her chin. "I'm serious, Ben."

His smile disappeared faster than a galleon caught in a hurricane. He started, then stopped himself. "The Museum of Maritime History signed off on our research."

She nodded. "Jay Bruce verified your research. He's no longer with the museum. In fact, several law-enforcement agencies have been trying to track him down. Seems he was selling bogus shipwreck information on the Internet." The crestfallen expression on Ben's face almost made her feel bad. "Almost" being the operative word.

"Why wasn't I notified?"

"You just were."

A vein throbbed in his neck, reminding Kayla he was human after all.

"Mr. Andrews was supposed to explain the details when the arrangements for my—" she searched for the correct word "—visit were made. I know you've been blindsided. I don't blame you for being...defensive, but the museum and investors are a bit concerned with the lack of targets, given the vast area you've searched."

"They said they were worried about the legitimacy of the operation."

"That, too," she admitted. "But funds are not unlimited."

Ben Mendoza might be a lot of things, but stupid wasn't one of them. The thoughtful look on his face told Kayla he understood the seriousness of the situation. She didn't want to threaten him, but would if necessary. Finding the *Isabella* was the priority. Nothing else mattered. Especially his overinflated ego.

"I stand by our research," he said. "We hired the top shipwreck researcher in the world to locate the *Izzy*."

"And you've been using this 'top' researcher's work for how many years? Two? Or is it three?"

Ben frowned.

Okay, maybe her last remark wasn't called for, but Ben didn't seem to realize she was one of the top shipwreck researchers. She was better than his guy. She'd spent her childhood following her father's work and learning all he had to teach. She always knew maritime history would be her lifework. Her father had told her the sea was in her blood, and she knew in her heart it was true.

"Even the most brilliant researchers are known to falter." Kayla smiled. "Present company excluded."

He didn't crack a smile. His lack of humor didn't surprise her. His lack of humor was the first thing that fell into line with her expectations. But no matter what she thought of him, they would have to work together.

Ben raised a brow. "What makes you so certain your research is correct?"

"The *Isabella* has been part of my life for as long as I can remember."

Her father used to tell her stories about the ship and

the pirates who'd sailed on her. She remembered the long hours he spent researching the lost shipwreck. The value of the cargo was unimaginable, but her father had located treasure ships before. This one had been different. For some reason, the *Isabella* held a greater allure for him. Kayla wished she understood why.

"I've studied and researched the *Isabella* off and on for the last eleven years." Ever since the submersible accident had taken her father's life and two others'. She ignored the empty feeling inside her and touched the silver talisman she always wore around her neck. It was the only key to her past, to the memory of the father she loved and the mother she couldn't remember. Kayla fought an unexpected rush of emotion. "It's taken a bit of digging and sorting through letters, journals, old charts and insurance records, but in the last two months I finally pulled all the information together to support my coordinates."

"And?"

"The *Isabella* was my father's obsession." She wasn't about to admit how important the pirate ship had become to her. No one knew how much she wanted to find the *Isabella*, and Kayla wanted to keep it that way. She hid the talisman under her shirt. "His research has proved invaluable to me and verifies my own."

"And?"

"My instincts." A satisfied feeling settled in the center of her chest. "I know I'm right."

His features hardened. "You're touting your so-called researching brilliance on a feeling?"

"An instinct," she corrected him.

"Same difference. Why not consult a psychic?"

"I did that, too." She smiled. "I figured it couldn't hurt."

His sharp gaze met hers, making Kayla want to step back. "How many expeditions have you been on?"

She stood her ground. She wasn't about to let him intimidate her. "Zero."

"Zero," he echoed. "This is your first time at sea?"

"Yes."

"That makes perfect sense." A glint of something—amusement, perhaps—flickered in his eyes. "The museum is worried about the legitimacy and spending habits of the expedition so they send you—a highly respected maritime historian who's never been on a search before and consults psychics and uses her instincts to locate shipwrecks."

The truth sounded a bit unusual, but at least Ben was finally seeing things clearly. She nodded.

"Yes, it makes perfect sense if we were looking for the *Izzy* in the Bermuda Triangle and Bigfoot was the captain of this ship and the sky was…purple."

Okay, so maybe he didn't quite get it. She'd have to go into more detail and—

Ben turned and walked down the hallway.

"Ben?" He didn't stop, so she did the next logical thing. She followed him.

The woman was a real…fruitcake. Ben had another word for her—several, actually—but he was watching his language, both verbally and mentally, for Madison's sake.

Another second of listening to the wacky historian and Ben would have lost it. So he walked away. She called after him, but he didn't consider glancing back.

Kayla might be a looker, but she was as nutty as they came. Might as well tie a bunch of helium-filled balloons on her and let her float around in the ozone because that's where she belonged—in the clouds with all the other dreamers. It was as if his father and Ben's ex-wife had been combined into one person named Kayla Waterton.

What had he done to deserve her?

Footsteps sounded behind him, but he kept walking.

"Where are you going?" Kayla asked. "I haven't given you the new coordinates."

As if he would ever use her coordinates. Ben continued down the passageway. Perhaps it was rude, but it would be ruder for him to speak. Neither she nor the museum would appreciate what he had to say. He wasn't about to let a few choice words jeopardize the expedition. He recognized a threat when he heard one. No Kayla, no funding. If only it were that simple...

His cabin door was open. A minicyclone had cut a path through the room and left devastation in its wake. Drawers hung open. Closet doors were ajar. Clothes lay strewn across the floor. He didn't need this right now. Ben stepped inside.

Madison sat on his bunk, her legs crossed and Baby Fifi on her lap. Fat tears streamed from her red-rimmed eyes and squeezed his heart. "I can't find the little magpie, Daddy."

"Come here, princess." Ben scooped her up into his arms and sat on the bed. She was the greatest treasure in his life. He wanted to be a good father and give her what he'd never had growing up: stability and security. Sometimes he succeeded, other times he needed to work harder. Much harder.

Madison buried her face against his chest. "Do you think the little magpie flew away?"

"She's right here."

The crying stopped. Madison looked around. "Where?"

He smoothed her hair. "Right here in my arms."

"I'm in your arms."

Ben smiled. "You're my little magpie."

Two small lines formed above the bridge of her nose. "I'm not a magpie, I'm Madison."

"Yes, you are. But you also repeat whatever I say. That's what magpies do." He lifted her into the air. "So that makes you my magpie Madison."

"Magpie Madison." She giggled, and a smile replaced the tears. Everything was right in her little world. And his, too. "Lift me up again, Daddy."

Ben did as he was told. Again and again and again. Nothing fun could be done only once.

"Hello," she said in midair. "This is my daddy's room. Do you want to play?"

Reality came crashing back. He glanced at the doorway. Kayla stood watching them, an odd expression on her face.

"Hello." A thoughtful smile formed on Kayla's lips. "You walked away so quickly I didn't know what was wrong. I forgot Madison had gone off by herself."

He weighed the situation. Madison wasn't the reason he'd walked away, but Kayla didn't know that. He still had to report to the museum. No doubt she would be in touch with it, too. He had to be smart about this. "She knows she's not supposed to go on deck by herself, but it's not good to leave her alone for too long. Usually she's back before I have a chance to worry."

"You worry?" Kayla sounded so surprised. "You don't look the type."

"I worry about things that are important to me."

"Want to see my room?" Madison asked her.

Kayla nodded. "I'd love to."

"I need to talk to Miss Waterton first. Go on ahead and she'll be right there."

"Okay, Daddy." With Baby Fifi in her arms, Madison stopped in the adjoining doorway to her cabin and turned. "I'm really happy you're here, Miss Water—"

"Call me Kayla. And thank you. I'm happy I'm here, too."

With a wide smile on her face, Madison danced into her cabin. Ben could see how much having another female aboard already meant to his daughter. If it were anyone but Kayla…

She motioned to the mess in his room. "I take it she tried looking for the little birdie."

"Yes." He brushed his hand through his hair. "Didn't think she'd look this hard, though."

"Shows her determination."

"Or her stubbornness."

Kayla winked. "Takes after you, does she?"

"Yes." A smile tugged at the edges of his mouth. Madison already liked Kayla. Maybe she wasn't so bad, after all. "Madison's mother claimed she was a DNA copy machine. Only hers got left out."

He picked up a pile of clothes and placed them on his bed.

"Where is Madison's mother?"

He shut a drawer and glanced up.

"You spoke about her in the past tense so I'm assuming she passed—"

"Last I heard she was in L.A." Bitterness coated the inside of his mouth like barnacles on the hull of his ship. Too bad it wasn't as easy to scrape away. "She's off chasing her dream of stardom."

"How often does Madison see her?"

"She doesn't." Ben closed another drawer, taking care not to slam it. He didn't know why Kayla wanted to know and resented the intrusion into his personal life. Still, he answered, "I have full custody. Her mother didn't want any visitations."

"Daddy," Madison called out. "Are you done playing with Kayla? I want my turn."

Ben smiled. "In a minute, princess."

Kayla's eyes gleamed with interest. "So it's just you and your daughter?"

He nodded, ignoring the little voice in his head calling him a failure. He'd failed to make his marriage work. Failed to provide his daughter with a stable family home. Failed to find the *Izzy*.

"My mother died when I was two so it was just my dad and me, too."

Ben noticed the past tense. "Your father?"

"He died eleven years ago right before my sixteenth birthday."

An orphan. The word seemed old-fashioned, but that's what Kayla was. He thought about Madison. At least she wouldn't be alone if something happened to him—his parents would care for her. "That must have been rough."

Kayla nodded. "Seeing you and Madison together brings back so many wonderful memories. I don't remember my mother, but my dad did an amazing job raising me on his own. He was the best."

Her love showed both in her voice and in her eyes. Ben hoped Madison grew up feeling the same way about him. Raising a daughter alone would only get harder as she got older. He wondered if Kayla had any regrets. "Did you miss having a female influence in your life?"

"Sometimes," she said. "Actually, a lot of times when I was a teenager. But I loved my dad so much. It had always been just the two of us. I assumed he would fall in love and remarry, and maybe if he had…'' Kayla got a faraway look in her eyes.

Her smile, full of honesty and openness, touched Ben in a way he'd never felt before. He wanted to reach out to Kayla, but couldn't. Something—make that lots of things—held him back. He looked away, shut the closet doors and straightened the photo on his nightstand.

She continued. ''If you do the best you can with Madison, you'll be fine. And so will she.''

He hoped so. Every day was a new adventure. Some good, some messy, some he never wanted to repeat. Soon Madison wouldn't be a little girl… His stomach knotted, and he picked up a shirt from the floor.

''And who knows—'' Kayla winked ''—you might find someone to share your life with one day.''

He tossed the shirt onto his bed with the other clothes. This conversation was getting too personal. ''We work a four-hour on, eight-off schedule. Do you want a shift?''

''I'd love one.'' Excitement sparkled in her eyes. ''Should I give the coordinates of the *Isabella*'s location to the captain or you?''

''We need to finish our current search first.''

Kayla's smile fell. ''But—''

''We'll discuss your coordinates later.'' If Ben had his way, later would never come. She would be out of here before then. ''Dinner's at 1800. Your shift starts at 0100.''

Her eyes widened. ''At 1:00 a.m.?''

''Is that a problem?''

''No,'' she said a little too quickly. ''It's fine. Great. Perfect.''

Ben smiled at her attempt to sound enthusiastic. He

couldn't wait to hear how she sounded in a couple of days when she said bon voyage. Those words would be music to his ears.

Kayla could handle this, she really could. The more times she told herself that, the better she felt. And things had gotten better over the past few hours.

Her tour of the ship, with its high-tech search capabilities and equipment, raised her hopes of finding the *Isabella*. The *Xmarks Explorer*'s facilities were first-rate. A STORM portable satellite terminal provided communication channels and data-exchange means and Internet access. She'd be able to keep in constant touch with the investors and the museum.

The crew was larger than she'd expected. One group dealt with the ship's operation and the other handled the search. She sighed at the thought of working with the bawdy crew of search-and-salvage "specialists" and eating meals with them.

As dinnertime rolled around, Kayla wasn't sure what to think. She sat alone at a small round table in the ship's dining room. Ben was the only one who didn't seem to be watching her eat, and that suited Kayla fine. If only she could stop noticing him, too. Despite his less-than-stellar personality, she liked seeing him interact with his daughter. And scowl or not, he was easy on the eyes.

Just like tonight's dinner was easy on Kayla's stomach. She leaned back in her chair and smiled. Stevie, a two-hundred-and-fifty-pound towering giant from Minneapolis, had cooked lasagna. Although, *cooked* didn't do justice to the delicious melted-cheese-and-veggie concoction that she might expect to be served at her favorite Italian restaurant back home in Portland, Oregon, rather than on a salvage ship in the middle of the Pacific Ocean.

Stevie carried a tray of sourdough slices. The aroma alone added calories. "More bread, Kayla?"

"No, thanks. I must have eaten half a loaf already. Did you make the bread from scratch?"

He nodded. "I use a starter my grammy gave me seven years ago. Sure you don't want another slice?"

"Maybe one more." As she took a piece, Stevie grinned, showing the gap between his front teeth.

"Yo, Cookie." A short, stocky man with reddish hair strutted up. "More bread over here."

She noticed Madison watching the interaction. This was none of Kayla's business, but the little girl was only three and very impressionable. She had to say something.

"Excuse me, but I forgot your name," Kayla said to the man.

"I'm Fitz." His green eyes danced. "Want to get to know me better? Say in the horizontal position?"

Stevie stared at his tray of bread.

"Thanks, but I'll pass." Kayla pasted on a smile and lowered her voice. "Right now I'm more concerned about Madison, who's listening to everything you say. Good manners are important, especially in front of a three-year-old."

Fitz's face reddened to match his curly hair. "Damn, I forgot about the kiddo."

Staring at the floor, Fitz shuffled back to his table.

Time would tell if he'd learned his lesson. Kayla finished a bite of bread. She'd died and gone to bread-lover's paradise. "Do you always cook like this?"

"Nah, I mean, no." Stevie said. "This is one of my lighter meals."

She'd have to pay attention to her eating habits on board. Food tended to go straight to her hips.

"I set out a pan of brownies if you're interested."

"Are doubloons gold?" Kayla joked. "I love brownies. I love anything chocolate."

"Chocolate is as necessary as oxygen and water," Stevie said. "I bake this amazing triple-layer devil's food cake with fudge icing."

"Okay, you're my new best friend." Kayla winked. "But I'm going to have to start working out or my appetite and your awesome cooking are going to get the best of me."

Stevie's smile widened. "A woman after my own heart."

"Why don't you take your heart and get back to work?" Ben said.

"Sure thing, boss." Stevie headed to another table.

Kayla looked up. Ben towered over her. His harsh gaze made her self-conscious. Still, she smiled. "Stevie seems nice."

Ben frowned. "Don't flirt with the crew."

Flirt? The idea was ludicrous. She rarely had time to date let alone perfect the art of flirting. Her life revolved around two things: researching shipwrecks and trying to find answers about her past. There wasn't room for anything more, especially a man. "I was only making conversation."

"You really don't get it."

What a shame he didn't treat everyone the way he treated Madison. Ben was attractive when he wasn't snarling like a caged tiger. "Get what?" Kayla asked.

"Stevie won't realize the difference."

"Stevie and I discussed food. Nothing else."

"Doesn't matter," Ben said. "He'll think you're interested in him."

She wasn't an idiot. And from what she'd seen so far, neither was his crew, despite the belching, bad manners and not-so-subtle stares. "I know how to deal with men."

"Not these men."

Kayla didn't like Ben's attitude. "What if I'm interested in Stevie?"

"What?"

She tried not to smile at his shocked tone. "It's not every day a woman finds a man who can cook like that," she whispered. "Is he married?"

"Stevie married?" Ben's frown turned into a scowl. The pirate was back. Dark and dangerous and more than a little peeved. "He's only twenty-four."

"I'm only twenty-seven. Besides, he might like older women." Kayla was enjoying herself, especially since Ben wasn't. "And what does age have to do with being married?"

Ben stared at her as if she'd lost her mind. "Are you...serious about this?"

She let him stew for a minute. She had the upper hand and she liked it. Liked it a lot. "That's none of your business."

His eyes darkened to an inky black. His lips narrowed until they almost disappeared. "Whatever happens on this ship is my business. Do you understand?"

She was playing with fire. Something she never did. But she'd never been on a ship with a band of pirates before. Time to take chances even if it meant getting burned. The crew and Madison were staring at them. Too late to back down now.

"Do you?" Ben repeated.

"Aye, aye, Captain." Kayla saluted him. "I read you loud and clear."

Chapter Three

Standing on the bow, Ben took comfort in the scents of saltwater and sunscreen and oil in the air. The familiar smells and daily routines gave the appearance of normalcy. But nothing was normal with Kayla Waterton aboard.

He wanted to know how her first shift had gone last night, but she was still asleep. She might sleep until her next shift. He didn't know. He knew nothing about her. Ben told himself he didn't care. He didn't. He was just getting…curious. And that bothered him. More than he wanted to admit.

Madison raced ahead of him in her Tweetybird sandals and pink life jacket. "Hurry, Daddy."

"The deck is wet," he said. "Don't run."

Beneath a cloudless blue sky, Madison kicked off her shoes. "Aye, aye, Captain."

Thanks to Kayla, Ben had heard that phrase a hundred times since last night. Even Madison had joined in.

"Who am I?" he asked.

"My daddy."

"That's right." He knew she was a smart kid. "I'm Daddy. Don't forget that."

"Aye, aye, Captain."

Maybe she was a little too smart, Ben realized.

Madison saluted him though her hand was at nose level. "Is this the right way, Daddy?"

He'd put his navy days behind him and wanted to keep it that way. "That's perfect, princess."

"Let's play." She plopped down in her plastic kiddie pool and kicked. The pool had been Wolf's idea and a great one at that. It kept Madison entertained for hours. The entire crew had gotten involved. Stevie set up a cooler and filled it with drinks and snacks. Monk put together a pump device to fill the pool with seawater. "You be the monster and splash me."

Ben did as ordered. Her squeal of laughter brought a welcome smile to his face. He needed to spend more time with Madison and less time thinking about the expedition and Kayla. He raised his arms and growled. "I'm going to get you."

"No, I'm going to get you." Madison splashed until he was soaking wet. She giggled. "You're all wet, Daddy."

"Yes, I am." He removed his shirt and tossed it on a nearby chair. "You got the best of the monster."

"Real monsters don't admit defeat so easily."

At the sound of Kayla's voice, he turned. "They do when facing a beautiful fairy princess," he said.

Kayla stood a few feet away from him at the top of the staircase leading to the bow. She wore a navy T-shirt with a schooner on the front and a pair of khaki shorts that showed off her long, tanned legs. Legs that went on forever. A dull ache spread through him.

A no-shorts-allowed rule would come in handy. No, the boys wouldn't go for that. Not in this great weather and with Kayla on board. Nothing was wrong with looking as long as everything else stayed professional. Yeah, Ben could live with that.

"I'm the princess and Daddy's the monster," Madison said. "Wanna be a princess, too?"

Playing did not constitute professional behavior in Ben's opinion. Nor did the urge to run his fingers through Kayla's hair. Each strand glistened like gold. No doubt he was catching treasure fever like the rest of the crew. He needed to stay focused. "Miss Waterton has work to do, princess."

"I have a few minutes to spare." Kayla walked toward him. Her hips swayed seductively. "And I'd love to be a princess, if I'm not intruding."

She was a siren. She had to be. Ben knew it wasn't his smartest move, but the expectant looks on both Kayla's and Madison's faces made it impossible for him to say no. At least they weren't playing house. Or doctor. "You're not intruding."

"Thanks," Kayla said.

Her soft smile tugged at his heart. Ben didn't like it. His heart was off limits to everyone but Madison. She pulled at his heartstrings enough. There wasn't room for anyone else.

"All princesses have to get in the water," Madison ordered. "Otherwise the monster will get you."

"Wouldn't want that to happen." Kayla kicked off her deck shoes and stepped into the pool. The water hit mid-calf. "Am I safe now, princess?"

Madison tilted her chin the same way Kayla had done a few times. "Sit down."

"I don't want to get my clothes wet. May I stand instead, Your Highness?"

Madison thought for a moment. "You may."

Kayla curtsied. "Thank you, princess."

"Get in the pool with us, Daddy." Madison waved her arm in the air as if she held a magic wand. "You can be the prince."

Ben stared at the pool. It was already crowded with Madison and Kayla. Besides, he knew princesses liked to dance with princes. At least his princess did. And if Kayla did, too...that would be far from professional. New rule—no dancing among crew members. "I like being the monster."

Amusement flickered in Kayla's eyes. "It's a fitting role."

Ben growled, "Thanks."

"Anytime." She glanced around the bow at the various chairs and loungers. "Nice little pool area."

Madison splashed water onto the deck. "It's my beach."

"We call it the beach," Ben said. "There's a cooler with drinks if you get thirsty and the bathroom is right over there."

Kayla nudged a beach ball to Madison. "Thanks."

Zach jogged up the stairs, grabbed a soda from the cooler and downed a swig. He let out a loud burp.

"Excuse you, Uncle Zach," Madison said.

His gaze fell on Kayla, and Zach blushed.

"Manners are important." Madison emphasized each word with a pointed finger. Three going on thirty. "Isn't that right, Kayla?"

Her smile had enough wattage to light a cruise ship. "That's right."

Zach muttered an apology and took the stairs two at a time.

Ben laughed. At least Kayla helped with the crew's lack of etiquette. Better manners were needed around here, but sometimes he had trouble remembering that himself.

"How did it go last night?" he asked.

Kayla rubbed water on her legs. "We didn't see anything."

She sounded nonchalant, but Ben heard a twinge of disappointment. "Nothing at all?"

"Not unless you want to count mud."

Frustration filled her voice. Bingo. He knew it wouldn't take long, but this was better than he'd hoped for. He bit back a smile.

Madison splashed him. "Can we play in the mud, Daddy?"

"Not today, princess."

She pursed her lips, but before a full-blown pout formed, she reached for her buckets and filled them with water from the pool.

Time to tighten the screws. "The *Izzy* is out there, Kayla. It's difficult when we have such a large area to search. An overdose of mud is one of the hazards."

"I know, but…" She shifted her weight between her feet.

This was it. She was going to give up after her first shift.

"Daddy, I have to go potty," Madison answered instead.

He helped her out of the pool. "Do you need help?"

"No, I'm a big girl." She ran into the head, located ten feet away, and closed the door.

"Sometimes she runs through the entire ship so she

can tell me she has to go. Kids.'' He studied Kayla, trying to figure out what was going on inside her pretty head. ''What were you going to say before?''

''I don't know how to tell you this…''

''No need to hold back now.''

''I suppose. It's just…I've only been here twenty-four hours, yet it seems longer.''

''I know.'' *Remain cool.* As soon as she said the word, he would radio Pappy to come back and get her. ''What's on your mind?''

Kayla squared her shoulders. ''We're wasting time and money with this current grid. I've spoken with the crew about your findings so far. None of the targets have panned out. Nothing confirms the *Isabella* went down in this vicinity. It's time we moved on.''

Yes, especially if the ''we'' meant only her.

He didn't like Kayla speaking with his crew, who were already on edge. Everyone believed the *Izzy* was out there, but Ben had heard rumblings of discontent about another wasted season. ''We have no idea how big the debris field is scattered.''

''Granted, but we're not going to find anything here.'' She rubbed her right foot on her left calf, and Ben forced himself to look away. This was not the time to be distracted. ''We can always come back later.''

''Later? Losing confidence in your research?''

''I'm still confident.'' She tilted her chin. At this moment, she looked like a real princess, not a pretend one. No wonder Madison had mimicked the action. ''We'll find the *Isabella* if we follow my research, so it's easy to say we can come back later.''

Ben appreciated Kayla's honesty. ''But if we don't, we won't be able to come back if our funding is pulled.''

''I could…put in a good word.''

How much pull could a historian have at the museum? Unless she was sleeping with the boss. No, he realized, she didn't seem the type. He glanced at the closed door to the head. Another minute and he'd have to check on Madison. "You think that will help?"

She rubbed her foot again. "It couldn't hurt. We all want the same thing."

"I want to find the *Izzy*."

"So do I." The determination in her voice surprised him. "But I can't find the *Isabella* without your ship and crew. And you can't find her without my research."

She'd been honest with him; she deserved the same. Kayla still hadn't offered to show him any real proof to back up her search coordinates. "I'm withholding judgment about your research."

"Whatever. You'll see I'm right."

He respected her confidence. Not that he believed her any more than he had yesterday. He might be on a treasure hunt, but he was relying on historical research and a scientific process to find it. Not intuition or feeling or psychics. Those three things his father would have trusted without a moment's hesitation in order to make one of his dreams come true.

"What matters is locating the ship." She circled the pool, kicking her feet as she walked. Her healthy tan suggested she spent time outdoors. The color was too natural-looking to be from a tanning booth or a bottle. "Who cares what research we use as long as we find her?"

This had to be a setup. Kayla sounded sincere, but he'd been mistaken about a person's sincerity before and wouldn't fall into that trap again. Still, he couldn't figure her out. She was either full of principle or stubborn, determined to get her way no matter what. Or maybe, he realized, a little of both.

"We need to work together."

Ben wasn't about to commit to anything except wanting her off his ship. "You want to work with me?"

"And the crew." Her eager smile made her look younger. "We're in this together."

She sounded like a high school cheerleader. All she needed were the pom-poms and a short little skirt. Ben liked the image forming in his head. But this wasn't a football game. No "rah-rahs" or "go team, go" cheers necessary. She wasn't part of his team. "We'll be done with this search soon."

Hope glimmered in her eyes. "And then?"

A beat passed. "We'll see."

Kayla didn't want to see. She wanted action.

Unfortunately, all she could do was wait. Wait for Ben to return from helping Madison in the bathroom. Wait for Ben to make a decision about the search coordinates.

"Hey, Kayla." Monk, the best-looking of the crew, with sun-bleached blond hair, clear baby-blue eyes and a sexy Southern drawl, sauntered over to the pool. He pulled his T-shirt over his head and winked. "Your turn, darlin'."

"You've got to be kidding."

"Fitz makes jokes around here." Monk's eyes twinkled. "I make love."

Kayla managed not to burst out laughing. She felt like the housemother of a fraternity, but somebody had to rein these fellows in for Madison's sake. "Can I ask you a question?"

"Anything, darlin'."

"Do you consider your behavior acceptable for a three-year-old to witness?"

He glanced around. "Madison isn't here."

"She's in the bathroom with Ben so she might be able to hear you. But that isn't the point. I'm sorry to lecture you, but do you want Madison to grow up believing this—" she pointed to his shirt on the deck and to him "—is how a woman should be treated by a man?"

"Hell, no." Monk grimaced. He picked up his T-shirt and put it on. "Aw, Kayla. I never thought about it that way. I'll do better. Really."

As Monk left the "beach," Kayla paced in the small pool. The saltwater made her legs feel better. A way they hadn't felt since coming on board. She must have hit the rail harder than she realized. But a few aches and pains were nothing to worry about when the expedition was on the line.

No question about it. Ben had to change course. It was her responsibility, her duty, to make that happen. She was going to tell Ben her true position at the museum and order him to go to her coordinates.

Madison ran back to the pool. "I went potty."

Kayla hadn't spent much time with children and didn't know the proper response. Clapping, cheering, a standing ovation? She decided on words. "You're such a big girl."

"Daddy had to help me wash my hands."

"You did most of the work," Ben said.

Madison grinned. "Because I'm a big girl."

Kayla glanced over at Ben and sucked in a breath. She'd experienced the same reaction when she climbed the small staircase to the bow and saw him sans shirt playing with Madison. Seeing his bare chest shouldn't be such a big deal. He was only a man. But her on-alert hormones and zinging nerve endings failed to appreciate that small detail.

Not that she blamed them.

The sun had deepened the color of his skin, and water from Madison's splashes glistened on his chest, arms and legs. He had more of a swimmer's than a body-builder's physique, without an ounce of flab. At least none she could see. And she'd been looking. Hard.

He picked his daughter up out of the pool. "You're my big girl, Madison."

His voice softened as he spoke Madison's name. Kayla wondered what it would feel like to have someone say her name like that. Her father used to, but to have a man like Ben say it with such unconditional love...she sighed. Not going to happen. At least not in the near future. She had too many questions about her past that needed answers before she could open her heart to love and family.

Ben spun Madison around. The little girl's giggles tickled Kayla's ears and made her feel warm and fuzzy inside. Children saw such joy in the littlest things. The idea of having a child of her own appealed to Kayla more than it ever had, but it still wasn't time.

She stepped out of the pool. A part of her wanted to join in on the fun. But the other part knew she didn't belong.

Ben stopped spinning and set Madison down. Kayla noticed a large scar on his back and a smaller one near his left shoulder. Ugly white gashes contrasted against Ben's dark skin. She couldn't imagine what had caused such terrible scarring.

"Come here, princess." Wolf appeared and called for Madison. Kayla noticed he'd tucked in his shirt and shaved. Maybe not all the crew was as uncivilized as she thought. "It's time for school."

"School. School. I love school." She skipped into the big man's arms. "Can I send an e-mail to Grandma and Grandpa?"

"Yes, and I bet they sent one to you." Wolf picked her up, not caring she was dripping wet. "See you at lunch, boss."

"Thanks." Ben watched Madison leave, his eyes filled with love. "We set up a daily preschool for Madison. The crew takes turns watching her, too."

"She's a lucky little girl to have all of you who love her so much."

"I'm the lucky one. Between Madison and my crew, I've got it made." He pointed at the water. "Did you see the dolphins?"

A pair of dolphins swam next to the ship. Jumping alongside the bow, the two put on an entertaining show. She envied their ability to swim so freely amid the waves and wondered what it would be like. She stood at the rail. "I've never seen a dolphin this close."

"It's an amazing sight." Ben approached her. "When I was a kid all I ever wanted to do was swim."

"I've never swum in the ocean." Another dolphin joined the pair and Kayla smiled. "My mother drowned in the water, and Dad worried about the same thing happening to me."

"I don't blame him."

His gaze caught hers. Time stopped. The noise from the engines faded into the background. In that instant, he wasn't a pirate. He wasn't a salvor. He wasn't a father. He was just Ben.

He looked away.

She was happy he did. He might be attractive—drop-dead gorgeous, to tell the truth—but that didn't matter. She wasn't here to find a boyfriend; she was here to find a ship.

And some answers.

Kayla scratched her feet. The sun had dried her skin, and her feet itched again. Her legs felt weird, too. Tight. Hot. She clutched the railing.

"You okay?"

"I'm fine."

As Ben leaned toward her, she caught a whiff of his scent—sea and soap with a little sunscreen mixed in. Nothing exotic or expensive. It was all Ben, and she liked it. A little too much.

Kayla sat in one of the plastic deck chairs. She needed to rest her legs. Maybe she'd gotten too much sun. Or too much Ben.

He kneeled at her side. "Do you need anything?"

You. Her stomach felt like a whirlpool, swirling around and around. She took a breath and exhaled slowly. "No, thanks."

"Your face is pale."

She shrugged it off, ignoring the concern in his voice. She didn't know which Ben—pirate or father—cared. For all she knew, he wanted to find a way to get rid of her.

Give the man a break. He's not that bad.

At least she hoped not.

She was having a hard enough time dealing with him. No matter how hard she tried, she didn't get him. She understood his love for his daughter, but the rest was a mystery. She had enough mysteries in her own life. She didn't need another one.

Kayla noticed the jagged scars on Ben's back again.

Whatever had happened to him must have been painful.
"How did you hurt your back?"

"An injury."

The way he shrugged off her question told Kayla he
didn't want to discuss it.

A minute of silence passed. She wished she could see
the dolphins and not Ben. An unfamiliar ache squeezed
her heart. Kayla reminded herself he was a pirate. He
would take what he wanted, then sail after the next prize.
She didn't want to care. But for some reason, she did.

"I was in the navy."

His voice was so quiet it took her by surprise. "Is that
how you got interested in salvage?"

"It got me started. I was a navy diver." He spoke
with a detached, almost eerie tone. "I got injured during
a dive."

"You don't have to—"

"There was an explosion."

"Those scars are…shrapnel?" The thought of Ben
underwater and injured made her nauseous. Her stomach
constricted. Kayla was relieved she was sitting.

"The hull collapsed. I'm not sure what got me. Probably a combination." His eyes clouded, and he looked
down at the water. "Took two surgeries to fix. One of
my buddies wasn't so lucky. He didn't make it out."

Regret laced his words. Kayla touched his arm. His
skin felt warm, his muscles hard beneath her palm. "I'm
sorry."

"It was a long time ago," he said.

Ben was solid, strong. Yet in his eyes she saw a softer
man, a gentler man. A father, a lover. She felt his shoulder tense. "It still hurts, doesn't it."

He didn't say anything. He didn't have to.

Her hand lingered longer than it should. She pulled

away and missed the contact. Missed his warmth. Missed him. Kayla ignored the impulse to touch him again. What was going on? Giving comfort was one thing. Simply liking the way he felt was another. "Did you leave the navy because of your injury?"

"No." A wry grin graced his lips. "It might not look pretty, but the docs repaired the damage. I could have re-upped, but I was ready to get out."

"Do you miss the navy?" she asked.

"No."

"That bad?"

He shrugged. "If duty called, I'd go back. But I prefer the civilian life. Taking orders is for the dogs."

Kayla wasn't surprised, but that wouldn't make her job any easier. She shifted in her chair. "You like being in charge?"

"Damn straight." His lips eased into a smile. "Being the boss is the only way to go. You know what you need to know, and if you don't, it's your own fault."

Uh-oh. He didn't know who she was or who really was in charge out here. Tell him, a voice screamed. But Kayla couldn't. Not yet. She knew the answer but asked, anyway. "So you never take orders?"

"Unless the orders come from Madison." His grin widened. "She's a better boss than the navy ever was. And a whole lot cuter, too. Though if she ever found that out…"

He stared directly into Kayla's eyes, and she felt light-headed. She cleared her dry throat. "Your secret is safe with me."

If only hers was as safe from him…

Chapter Four

Sitting in the ship's lounge, Kayla stared at the rolls of sonar printouts spread out on the table. No targets with "cultural value" had been located yesterday, so they were reviewing old data rather than discussing what targets to reexamine. She was a researcher, not a sonar expert, but maybe she could see something the others had missed. Whatever the results, she needed to be doing something more productive than sunning herself on the "beach."

"Look at this one," Vance, an archeologist, said. "A debris field surrounds the center mass. We thought this was a geographic formation, but it was a ship."

Kayla studied the image. With thousands of shipwrecks littering the ocean bottom, Ben had stumbled on a few during his search. She wished one of them had turned out to be the *Isabella*. That would have made her life so much easier.

"See the hull." Gray, a sonar specialist with a dimpled smile, outlined the shape. "We sent the ROV down for a closer look. The wreck was too long. Not to mention steel.''

She glanced up at the two men. Kayla liked being part of the target discussion group. It made her feel as if she fit in and was a real member of the crew. ''Do you think the *Isabella*'s buried in sand where we can't see her?''

Vance rubbed his goatee. ''Part of her might be covered with sediment, but we should be able to tell if it's the *Izzy*. They found the *Central America,* so there's hope for other wood-hulled ships lost in deep waters.''

Eugene entered the lounge and handed her another roll of sonar scans. ''Here's more data, Kayla.''

Eugene pulled out a chair and sat across from her. A sweet young man with puppy-dog eyes and a crooked smile, he was a computer wiz who was writing a software program to ease the recording of sonar search data and information. ''We heard you know where the *Isabella* went down.''

Kayla stiffened. Answering might not be in her best interest. Ben's, either. Tension filled the silence. ''I, uh…''

Vance frowned. ''If you know something…''

''The boss hates not knowing everything.'' Gray's concern and warning was clear. ''If you're keeping it secret—''

''I've discussed this with Ben.'' She struggled with the correct words to say and ignored the shiver Gray's words sent down her spine. She didn't like secrets, either. But in this case, she'd had no choice. Kayla knew she wasn't wanted here. She'd withheld the truth to avoid a power struggle. She didn't want to make it worse. ''He knows I've done a lot of research on the *Isabella*.''

"So if you know where the *Izzy* sank, why haven't we found her?" Eugene asked.

"It's a little complicated." To say the least.

Stevie appeared with a plate of cookies. "Chocolate chip. Fresh from the oven."

Death by chocolate sounded great right now. She grabbed one and took a bite. The warm cookie melted in her mouth. "Delicious."

Stevie walked away with a big grin on his face.

Vance looked Kayla in the eye. The intensity made her shiver again. "You either know where the *Izzy* is or you don't."

Another bite. Thank goodness Stevie had left the plate. Cookies worked better than her breathing exercises. And she couldn't talk with her mouth full. Vance stared her down. She swallowed the cookie. Enough was enough. She disliked Ben pulling his he-man, dangerous pirate act on her, but Kayla wasn't going to allow anyone else to do it. "I know."

"Trying to rally support for a mutiny, Kayla?" Ben moved toward the table. The lounge seemed much smaller with him in the room. He towered over them as if he owned the place. Which he did, she realized.

He pulled up a chair and straddled it. "So what questions are you answering?"

She wiped her mouth. "Questions about the *Isabella*."

"Kayla has thoroughly researched the *Izzy*," Eugene said.

"She's not the only one." Ben's tone set her nerves on edge. Was he this way with everybody or just her? "Pirates and lost treasure are hot topics these days."

A warning bell rang in Kayla's head. "This is a scientific expedition." Everyone at the table nodded, but she wasn't convinced. "Of course, if we find any of the treasure, that's icing on the cake."

"Hell, that *is* the cake." Vance laughed. "Let's hope those pirates on the *Izzy* pillaged and plundered every ship in the Pacific."

Even Vance, a trained marine archeologist, had caught treasure fever. History showed how gold could drive even the sanest of men insane. "Luis Serrano might not have seized every ship in the Pacific, but he did his fair share of damage before the *Isabella* sunk."

"Who?" Gray asked.

"The pirate captain of the *Izzy* who stole all the treasure we're looking for," Ben answered.

"Luis Serrano de Martin," Kayla said at the same time.

Visions of gold danced in Gray's eyes. "Was he a bad dude?"

"He was a man obsessed," Kayla said.

Ben nodded. "By treasure."

"And love." Kayla's gaze collided with Ben's. His dark eyes hypnotized her and seemed to read her every thought. It was disconcerting, yet exciting. She wanted to keep their relationship professional, yet the way her blood coursed through her veins was anything but work-related. She forced herself to get back to business. "Luis raided ships sailing the Manila-Acapulco routes in order to marry Ana Delgado."

"She was supposedly one hot babe."

Kayla didn't like hearing Ben speak that way about another woman—even one who had been dead for a couple of centuries. A paddle wheel churned up her stomach. "How do you—"

"Research." He smiled a little too smugly for her

liking. "I did a little of my own before we set out to find the *Izzy*."

"Got any pictures, boss?" Gray asked.

"They didn't have any cameras back then," Eugene said.

Kayla was on a ship with men, but with the exception of Ben, she hadn't felt like the odd woman out until now. She wanted to play, too. "Too bad there weren't cameras, because I read Luis Serrano was a tasty piece of eye candy."

Ben raised a brow. "Eye candy?"

He looked wicked and sexy. Too male for her own good. Kayla shrugged. "Hot babe?"

"Facts are facts," Ben said.

And this conversation needed to get back on track. She slipped into her lecturer persona. All she needed was an overhead projector and a pointer. "The facts about Luis are interesting. He was the fifth son of a duke and left Spain in disgrace after being wrongly blamed for losing his galleon and several others during a storm and pirate attack. He joined up with a privateer and turned to pirating."

Ben nodded. "He wanted revenge against Spain for stripping him of everything from his name to his ship."

He had done his homework, and Kayla was impressed. She might question some of his decisions, but she liked his thoroughness. And a few other things, a little voice whispered.

"Where does the hot babe come in?" Vance asked.

Kayla tucked a strand of hair behind her ear. "Luis was sailing in the Pacific when he met and fell in love with Ana Delgado."

"You make it sound so romantic," Ben said.

Kayla straightened in her chair. "It was."

He snickered. "He seized her ship and held her captive."

If Luis were half the man Ben was, Kayla wouldn't have minded. She could imagine worse things. A heat built low in her belly. "Luis kept her safe until he returned Ana to her father in California. If he'd treated her badly, she wouldn't have fallen in love with him."

Ben laughed. "One of these days, I'd like to pay a visit to your little world. I'm sure it's very interesting there."

Kayla ignored him. "She fell in love with Luis, and he with her. But Ana was engaged to a Spanish nobleman. She begged her father to allow her to marry Luis instead. He wouldn't agree because Luis didn't have enough fortune or any means other than pirating to support his daughter. Luis decided to head back to sea to bring back a fortune worthy of Ana. She begged him not to go because she would make her father change his mind, but Luis didn't believe her and set sail."

"He was only doing what he had to do," Ben said.

His gaze locked on hers once again, and Kayla's breath caught in her throat. She imagined Luis Serrano looking exactly like Ben Mendoza. "Luis should have stayed, because a week later Ana convinced her father to let her marry him. But he was already gone, and all she could do was wait for his return."

"So the guy was a little impatient and he didn't want to wait around."

"It was more than that." Kayla wished she knew what the pirate had been thinking when he stayed at sea for so long. "Luis amassed a fortune in treasure. Gold, silver, porcelain and precious stones. He seized ship after ship. No amount of treasure was enough. He was out of control. Obsessed.

"Months passed and his crew convinced him to sail back to California. But the seasons had changed and they hit a storm."

"Luis went down with the ship," Ben said.

"But two crew members survived." Kayla had found notes in her father's research about them. "They said people from the sea helped them until a ship picked them up."

"Sea people?" Ben asked.

"Mermaids."

He rolled his eyes. "You sure it wasn't little green men?"

"No, they were too busy doing flybys over Roswell."

Ben laughed. She liked the sound. No, she didn't. Kayla clenched her fist under the table. No doubt he was laughing at her again.

He picked up a pen from the table and twirled it with his fingers. "Luis should have given one of those mermaids a shiny bauble or peso so he could have lived."

"Maybe he did." Kayla wanted to know what happened, but she hadn't found any information about the fate of Ana Delgado. "Maybe Luis showed up on Ana's doorstep and they lived happily ever after. I like that ending better than having her spend her entire life alone mourning Luis's death."

"He deserved to be mourned." Hurt flashed in Ben's eyes. "He died trying to win her love."

"He already had her love." Kayla tilted her chin. "Luis should have trusted Ana and their love. He should have listened to her and stayed. Warmed up to the father and showed him how much he loved his daughter."

"I would have stayed," Eugene said.

Vance and Gray agreed. Funny, until Eugene spoke,

Kayla had forgotten the other three men were there. Her focus had been totally on Ben.

"She never gave him reason to trust her," Ben said.

"He needed a reason?" Kayla had never been in love, but she knew how she wanted matters of the heart to work. "She gave him her promise, her word, her love. Just one of those things should have been enough."

Ben shrugged.

"What would you have done in Luis's place?" Kayla asked.

"Not fall in love in the first place." Ben made it sound as if love could be flicked on and off with a switch. No wonder he was divorced. "He should have ransomed Ana to her father or fiancé, got his money and sailed away."

Ben sounded like such a guy. Disappointment shot through Kayla. "That's horrible."

"It's real life." His eyes narrowed. "You never mix business with pleasure."

She never believed it would happen. At least not in her lifetime. Kayla laughed.

"What?" Ben asked.

"We finally agree on something."

Ben didn't care whether they agreed on anything or not.

Two days later, he stormed down the passageway. In the short time she'd been aboard, Kayla Waterton hadn't simply won over his crew. She'd turned the *Xmarks Explorer* into a ship of fools. She'd taken a group of lewd yet entertaining men and turned them into panting and primping poodles with little bows tied on their ears.

Fights for showers before dinnertime. A run on razor blades. The toxic mixture of aftershave lotions and colognes in the air. A battle to see who got to sit with her at meals. The sudden interest in folklore and fairy tales, two of Kayla's favorite subjects. Not to mention the emphasis on proper etiquette.

Maybe they'd been at sea too long. How else could he explain grown men acting like a litter of love-starved puppies lapping up whatever attention Kayla gave them?

He had to do something. Fast.

A pack of distracted puppies was useless to him.

"Hey, boss." Monk rushed by, nearly knocking Ben over. "Do you have an iron?"

The insanity continued. "This isn't a cruise ship. We don't dress for dinner."

"I don't care about dinner, but Kayla…" He blew out a puff of air. "She's one classy lady. Highly educated. Refined tastes. Definitely the nonwrinkle type. Hence my need for an iron."

Hence? Next thing, Monk would be spouting Shakespearean sonnets. Now, that would be scary.

"Classy, educated." Ben raised a brow. "Doesn't sound like your type."

A first-rate ocean geologist with a Ph.D., Monk was also the crew's resident ladies' man who lived by a "love 'em and leave 'em before they got your last name" motto. With surfer-dude blond hair and clear blue eyes, he got away with it thanks to his Southern drawl, farm-boy charm and movie-star good looks. "Come on, boss. You saw her wet. Talk about hot."

Yes, *hot* described a soaking-wet Kayla in her clinging pants and transparent T-shirt. Hell, it would describe her wearing a flannel nightgown that covered everything but her hands and head. Didn't matter. She was still trouble with a capital *T*. "Kayla's attractive."

"I told the guys you weren't immune to her—" Monk

nudged Ben with his elbow "—charms. Want in on the action?"

This was worse than high school and the navy combined. "What action?"

Monk winked. "The get-Kayla action."

Just when Ben thought it couldn't get worse... Hadn't he warned Kayla? Time to put a stop to this. "While Kayla Waterton is on board, she is a member of this crew. Not some bimbo you want to nail."

"I know that, boss. So do the other guys." Monk sounded almost earnest. A surprise, since *earnest* was one adjective Ben never associated with the man. "We're not talking about hooking up with Kayla. We're talking marriage. You know, a permanent arrangement."

Marriage was a four-letter word to all of his crew, including himself. The only good things about weddings were an open bar and free food. Ben smiled. "You had me going there for a minute."

"I'm serious, boss."

Ben didn't believe him. "You always said marriage was for wimps, wusses and women."

"That was before."

"Before what?"

"Before Kayla." Monk said her name with a reverence reserved for sports and supermodels. "I can now break my life into two halves. Before Kayla and after Kayla."

Ben was going to be sick.

"If you want in on the action, give Wolf a hundred. But you two haven't hit it off so I wouldn't waste your money." Monk raised a brow. "Though it would be a challenge."

Ben had already learned an important lesson. Challenge plus women equaled three things—disappointment, ulcer and divorce. "I'll pass."

"Smart move." Monk grinned. "I've got to find an iron before my shift starts."

Ben knew better, but he had to ask. "What are you going to iron?"

"My T-shirt. Impressions are everything." Monk waved. "Later."

Not if Ben could help it.

Time to put an end to this Kayla love-fest before disaster struck. If a confirmed bachelor like Monk was talking the m-word without any verbal threats or physical force being applied, what would the rest of the boys be thinking? This went beyond poker games and other forms of gambling the guys did to pass the time. This was entering a realm that could destroy the camaraderie of the crew—a crew more like family than employees—and keep them from finding the *Izzy*.

As he continued along the hall, his mind raced. He had to get Kayla off the ship. So far she hadn't complained about her shifts, the crew, nothing. His plan to make her want to go home wasn't working, which meant one thing. He needed a new plan.

Wolf stuck his head out of his cabin. "Hey, boss, can I ask you something?"

"What?"

Wolf opened the door and placed his hands on his stomach. "Do you think I need to go on a diet?"

"Not you, too."

"What?"

"Next you'll want to know if your jeans make your butt look too big."

Wolf glanced at his backside. "Do they?"

Ben covered his ears with his hands and walked away. "I'm not hearing this."

The others he could understand. Well, almost understand. Even he had to admit Kayla was a babe.

But Wolf, too? No way, no how. Ben's oldest and closest friend wasn't going to be taken in by a pretty face, a nice smile and a great set of...

Okay, Wolf had always been a breast man, but he was beyond this does-she-like-me-or-not high school behavior. Sensible, levelheaded. He was a rock. Ben's rock. Wolf had been his best man and was Madison's godfather. He'd seen Ben through his surgeries and recovery, his marriage and divorce, the opening of his salvage operation and now the raising of Madison. Wolf wasn't the kind of guy to be worried about love handles and the size of his butt. Hell, no man was that kind of guy.

Just shoot me now. And stop the insanity before it gets any worse. He needed to escape. Not an easy thing to do miles from land. Luckily he knew one place of sanity left on the ship—Madison's cabin.

Her door was ajar. Two female voices drifted out. Something about French braids and ponytails? Giggles followed and then a soprano, very feminine version of the ABC song.

He glanced in. Ribbons and barrettes and rings and bracelets lay on the floor. He counted two hairbrushes, three combs and half a dozen scarves in varying shades of pink.

With a seashell necklace around her neck, Kayla sat on the twin bed with Madison's bare feet on her lap. Madison wore a rhinestone tiara on her head and had every necklace she owned minus the shell one draped around her neck.

She flapped her hands in the air like a little bird. "Are they dry?"

"Not yet." Kayla held up two bottles of nail polish. "What color do you want on your toenails?"

"Pink. Purple." Madison stopped flapping. "No, pink."

Kayla's smile captivated him, and Ben felt an odd twinge in his stomach. He should let them know he was here, but he enjoyed watching them. Ben didn't have any sisters. He didn't know a lot about girly stuff and needed to learn for Madison's sake.

"It's hard to make up your mind sometimes, isn't it?" Kayla asked.

Madison nodded. She scrunched her forehead as if debating the fate of the world, not the color of nail polish. "I don't know which one to choose."

In that moment, Ben saw the future. Decisions about how to fix Madison's hair, what clothes to wear, what boys to… Ben wasn't ready for any of that. He wanted Madison to stay little forever.

"We can use both colors," Kayla suggested.

Good answer. No matter how he might feel about Kayla's presence on the ship, she'd been great to his little girl.

"Use both?" A brilliant smile erupted on Madison's face as she realized what Kayla meant. "I want this foot pink and this one purple."

Ben wanted to tell Madison to say please. As Kayla had been telling the crew, manners were important no matter what age. The sooner Madison learned that, the better. He ignored the inner voice reminding him eavesdropping wasn't polite.

"Let's do it." Kayla opened a bottle of nail polish and started painting.

Madison giggled. "That tickles my foot."

"I'm sorry." Kayla's voice was so soft and soothing. She had spoken to him that way when she'd asked about his injury and he'd liked it as much as Madison seemed to. "Do you want me to stop?"

Madison leaned her head back and her smile widened. "No, thank you. I like being tickled. My daddy tickles me."

Kayla finished painting the right foot, put away the pink bottle and opened the purple one. "Sounds like fun."

Madison sat straighter. "Daddy could tickle you."

Way to go, princess. Ben smiled. Tickling Kayla would add a new and welcome dimension to the age-old game.

"That would be..."

He could think of a whole lot of different words to insert—fun, intense, foreplay.

"Interesting," Kayla said finally. She continued painting Madison's nails. "But I don't like being tickled."

Bummer. Ben wondered why she didn't like to be tickled.

Two little lines appeared above Madison's nose. "Why?"

Kayla shrugged. "Just don't. I'm all done with your toenails. Do you like them?"

"Oh, yes. Thank you." Madison wiggled her toes. "They're so pretty."

"Just like you." Kayla laughed. "But sit still so they can dry and then you can paint mine."

Madison's eyes widened. "Really?"

Kayla nodded. "I'll show you how."

Adoration filled Madison's eyes. "I'm glad you're here."

Unguarded emotions played on Kayla's face. She kissed the top of Madison's head. "Me, too."

Two little words, but important ones for his daughter. The look of pure joy on her face warmed Ben's heart.

"Do you want to hear a story?" Kayla asked.

"I love stories." Madison scooted closer to her. "What's it about?"

"A fairy and how her dreams come true."

It was only one story, but still... Every one of Ben's nerve endings went on alert. His muscles tensed. Madison was so young and she wanted to believe in everything. Real or make-believe. Kayla had already shown him what a dreamer she was, and he couldn't allow her to influence his daughter that way.

As Kayla began with "Once upon a time," Ben turned away from the doorway and sagged against the wall. This was another complication, another distraction he didn't need. His crew might be falling for Kayla, but so was Madison.

She longed for female interaction, a mother figure, so to speak.

He didn't want Madison to get hurt, but worse, he didn't want her head filled with dreams. She was too young, too impressionable. He didn't want her heart broken.

Between Madison and his crew, no leeway existed. Kayla had to leave before she did any more damage. And Ben finally knew how to make that happen.

Chapter Five

Kayla stood at the stern of the ship, a safe distance away from the winches and hoists used to raise and lower the sonar sled, remotely-operated vehicles and submersible. The mixture of oil, diesel and salt in the air appealed to her, as did the well-used appearance of the gear, some of which had seen better days, because this was a working ship, not a pleasure vessel. And that fact alone gave her hope all was not lost. Hard work always paid off. Her father had shown her that.

She stared at the cables lying on the deck until they disappeared into the water. Sonar devices were attached to the submerged end of the cables thousands of feet down. She'd spent her afternoon shift staring at monitors displaying images from the ocean bottom. Nothing but mud—make that sediment. Either way, she'd wasted four more hours. At least this section of the Pacific would be mapped. But that didn't make her feel better.

How long before Ben realized the futility of his search?

Kayla had to convince him to go to her coordinates. She wasn't a quitter, yet she was discouraged, frustrated and a whole lot of other things. Her gut told her to take charge. To forget about what Ben Mendoza might think and take over the expedition. It wasn't only her right, but her responsibility. She owed that much to the museum, the investors and, most important, her father.

Touching the talisman around her neck, she stared at the shimmering water below. The dark blue contrasted with the whitecaps of the waves. The water called to her, beckoned her to jump in. She longed to feel the saltwater on her skin and swim like the dolphins she'd seen earlier. The impulse made little sense, but she believed people put too much weight on things that made sense. People like Ben.

Something hissed behind her. Kayla turned from the railing.

Ben stood next to a pump with a can of WD-40 in his hand. "Looking for anything in particular?"

"Just the *Isabella*."

"You look tired." He sprayed a gear. "Long day?"

The longer they searched Ben's grid, the longer the days would get. She nodded.

"I thought about what you said earlier." Ben's gaze met hers. "About finding the *Izzy*."

This was it. He was going to ask for her coordinates. She forced herself to remain calm, though her insides shook.

"The most important thing is finding the ship," he said. "Not who's right. Or wrong."

Kayla wanted to hug him. She smiled instead. "Exactly."

"I want to make a deal."

As he moved toward her, she stepped back and bumped into the rail. "Deal?"

"I agree to follow your search coordinates if you agree to leave."

"Leave?" Realization dawned and with it a hundred questions. She started with the two most obvious. "Leave the ship? The expedition?"

He nodded.

"But why?" Her voice cracked. She couldn't help herself. "Did I do something wrong?"

He looked away. "Not really."

"Not really?" Her blood pressure shot upward. "What's that supposed to mean?"

He checked a cable but said nothing.

She placed her hands on her hips. "I have a right to know."

He stared at her, but she could read nothing in his dark eyes. "You do."

She didn't feel any relief. Especially when he handed her the can of lubricant. "Hold this for me."

Kayla did. She wasn't about to be told she didn't take orders well. Not like some people.

Ben thanked her and adjusted the knobs on what she thought was a hydraulic pump.

She stared at the equipment as if it were the most fascinating piece of machinery she'd ever seen. At least she wasn't staring at Ben and waiting for him to speak. Kayla wanted to hear what he had to say, but she didn't want to appear anxious. She ground the toe of her shoe into the deck.

Finally he finished with the machine and gave it a loving pat. "Good as new."

Well, she wasn't. Kayla was losing patience. "Tell me now."

He pulled a rag from his pocket and wiped his hands. "I want you to leave."

"*You* want me to leave?"

He checked another gauge. "I do."

"Why?"

"Family."

She shoved the can into his hand. "You've lost me."

"Having you aboard is a distraction to my family."

"Madison is a little girl." Kayla didn't understand what was going on. "She's distracted by everything."

"She's getting attached to you."

"I'm already attached to her."

"She's highly impressionable."

"I know that."

"She doesn't understand the difference between reality and fantasy. If you tell her stories, she'll believe them."

"Isn't that wonderful?" Kayla smiled. "The world is full of all sorts of possibilities for her. I wish more people could view the world like a three-year-old."

He frowned. "I don't want her head filled with nonsense."

"Nonsense?"

"Fairy tales and dreams. Stuff like that."

"Why not?"

"I have to look out for her." Ben sounded upset. Angry. "I don't want her to get hurt."

Kayla didn't understand the reasoning behind his concern, but she knew he wanted only to protect his daughter. That appealed to her on a gut level and made Ben more attractive. The attraction went beyond his good looks and larger-than-life aura. It went deeper, to who he was as a man and a father. "I know you're concerned about Madison, but you're wrong about my hurting her.

Every time I see her, it's all I can do not to pick her up and smother her with love. She's this ray of sunshine who gives out bubble-gum flavored kisses and sticky-hand hugs.''

Ben simply stared at Kayla, his features tight. She wasn't about to give up.

"You don't know me, but I would never hurt your little girl. I couldn't.''

"Not on purpose.''

It wasn't the answer she wanted, but she'd take it. "Thank you for that. If I promise to be more careful around Madison, may I stay?''

"It's not only Madison. My family includes the crew—''

"I get along with every member of this crew. They've gone out of their way to be nice and make me feel like one of them.'' Not counting Ben, Kayla realized. "And I haven't been telling them any stories. If you're looking for an excuse—''

"The guys have a bet going about who will be the one to marry you.''

She swallowed. Hard.

"I've handpicked my crew. We've been together a long time. They're family. I can't have it all ruined because of—''

"Me,'' she said.

"A bet,'' he said at the same time. "A bet like this could cause real problems. The guys are competitive enough, and if this got out of hand... Do you understand?''

"Yes.'' And she truly did. Ben cared about his crew. He was looking out for them. She respected that. But it made her position more difficult. "Don't I have a say in any of this? Your crew may want to marry me, but I don't want to marry any of them. No offense intended.''

"None taken," Ben said. "I'm not part of the bet."

"I never thought you were." Kayla said the words a little too quickly and hoped he didn't notice. "This isn't fair."

"No, but it's a business decision." The finality of his tone sealed her fate like a judge's gavel declaring a life sentence. "I have to look out for my crew's best interest. If there was another way…"

"Would you let me stay?"

He stared at the horizon. The sun descended in the reddening sky. She remembered an old saying. Red sky at night, a sailor's delight. Tomorrow would be a nice day. It had to be better than the storm raging right now.

"Yes," he said finally.

Kayla wasn't about to celebrate. His hesitation told her this might go deeper than family and business, but she had bigger problems at the moment. Leaving the ship was unacceptable.

"So you'll leave."

Kayla noticed it wasn't a question. She had to find a way to stay. And she had very little time to do it. An idea popped into her head, but she wasn't sure if it would work or if she could pull it off. If it backfired… What choice did she have? "If you agree to use my coordinates, and we can't find a way to resolve this problem with your crew, I will leave."

Ben cracked a smile.

Unbelievable. She'd protected his feelings by keeping her true role in this expedition a secret, when he was trying to get rid of her. A knife in the back would have been subtler. Ben was a pirate in every sense of the word.

"Deal." He extended his arm. "Let's shake on it."

Shaking hands with the enemy didn't appeal to her, but he gave her no choice. As his large hand engulfed hers, an electric shock pulsated up the length of her arm. His grip was firm. Not too strong. Just right. His calloused skin was rough, yet warm. The handshake lingered. Lasted longer than it should have, given the circumstances. Now wasn't the time to get friendly. Kayla jerked away.

Two could play at this game. The rules had changed. No more playing nice. It was her turn, and the gloves were coming off.

Kayla didn't have time to be going to the bow right now. Her fate and that of the expedition rested in her hands. But Madison had wanted her to come, and Kayla didn't have the heart to say no.

"We have to hurry." Holding onto Baby Fifi, Madison climbed the steps on her tiptoes. "It's almost dinnertime."

"Why are you whispering?"

"Shh." Madison placed her finger at her lips. "We have to be really quiet or we'll scare the mermaid away."

Memories of waiting for a mermaid to appear came back to Kayla. She'd begged her father to let her go into the ocean and find one, but he wouldn't let her go near the water. She remembered her promise to Ben about being more careful around Madison, but his concern seemed more of a ruse to get her to leave. Dreams and fantasies were as normal as breathing for a young child. Still, she wouldn't encourage her, for Ben's sake. Kayla smiled. "Is there a mermaid nearby?"

Madison nodded. "I saw it before you came on the ship."

Kayla walked on her tiptoes, too. "Where?"

"In the water." Madison kneeled by the railing and motioned for Kayla to join her. "We have to be quiet so he doesn't know we're here. That's how Baby Fifi and me saw him before."

"Him?"

Madison nodded. "It was a daddy with a tail."

"A man like your daddy?"

She nodded. "He had dark hair like my daddy's and it was wet."

"What did he look like?" Kayla asked.

"He had pretty blue eyes. My daddy says I have pretty eyes, too, but mine are brown." Madison tilted her chin. "I know all my colors."

"Good for you."

"The mermaid was really tanned. He must've forgot to put on his sunscreen."

Kayla smiled at Madison's disapproving tone. "Did he say anything to you?"

"No, but he waved." Madison waved, even though no merman was there to wave back. "I saw his tail when he went under the water. It was gold and shiny like my daddy's earring."

She spoke as if it were the most normal thing in the world to have a merman wave to her. Kayla wanted to give Madison a great big hug. Kayla also wanted to have a talk with Ben about the importance of imagination. Madison's imagination needed to be fostered, not smothered. "Do you know what you saw?"

"Daddy said it had to have been a big fish. Maybe a whale. But whales are really big. He wasn't that big."

Figures Ben would say something like that. Kayla

sighed. "I suppose a merman might qualify as a big fish."

"A merman." Madison's eyes lit up. "My daddy said mermaids—mermans—aren't real. They exist in our *imanations.*"

"Mermaids exist in our imaginations and in our dreams."

"Have you ever seen one?" Madison asked.

"No, but my father told me stories about them." Kayla smiled at the cherished memories. "Would you like to hear one?"

"Yes."

She placed her arm around Madison's small shoulders. "A long time ago in a sea far, far away, a magical island called Atlantis existed."

Kayla told the same story her father used to tell her. She couldn't believe how much she remembered, and when she reached the end, Madison snuggled against her. "Can I hear it again?"

Kayla remembered how she'd felt when she was younger. She'd always wanted to hear the story again. And again. And again. "How about at bedtime?"

"Okay." Madison hugged Baby Fifi. "I like that story."

"Me, too." The Atlantis tale about mermaids had been her favorite and had gotten more complex as she got older. But Kayla had simplified the tale for Madison. The way her father had done for her when she was a little girl.

Daddy.

Kayla carried his memory in her heart, but she missed him and his stories so much. Some children had a favorite stuffed animal or blanket they carried with them and slept with; she'd had her father's stories. Those were her "loveys." He'd told her tales right until he set out on that fateful expedition and didn't return home.

"Do you know more stories?" Madison asked.

Kayla nodded. "My father told me lots of stories. I'd be happy to share them with you if we ask your daddy first."

"Okay." Madison stared at the water. "I wanted you to see the mermaid man, but I don't think we're going to see him now."

Kayla gave her a squeeze. "Don't worry, sweetie, we'll have plenty of chances to see him."

She was going to make sure of it.

Dinnertime rolled around. So far, no blood had been spilled over the fight for Kayla's affection, though the shooting-dagger glances being exchanged between Zach, Stevie and Fitz, who had snagged seats at Kayla's table, and the rest of the crew weren't making Ben feel that relieved. The three other men at his table stared longingly at the trio sitting with Kayla across the room.

She rose from her chair and tapped a spoon against her water glass. The clinking sound wasn't necessary. Her standing had silenced the room. "I want to make an announcement."

She was going to say goodbye. Ben sat back in his chair to enjoy the moment.

"Before dinner, I went to the control room and spoke with Gray and Vance. So they've heard what I'm about to say."

Each of his men focused their full attention on Kayla. Fitz grinned like a child. Zach almost drooled. Stevie rushed in from the kitchen and nearly took out the cart for the dirty dishes. Monk leaned over the table as if narrowing the distance between him and Kayla. Wolf held Madison on his lap and smiled like a fool.

Ben had never seen anything like it. Kayla had turned his crew into a bunch of pathetic blubbering idiots. A good thing she was leaving.

"Working with you guys is so much fun. You've made me feel at home." She looked each one of his crew in the eye, everyone except him. "I'm so lucky I've gotten to meet you all."

Ben saw the chests expanding and the egos inflating. Not what he needed. But hey, she was saying goodbye. He couldn't complain.

"But something's come to my attention." She paused and looked at each of the men again. "We need to address it and put a stop to it or I'm going to have to leave."

Eugene went pale. "Leave?"

"Over my dead body." Monk picked up a knife.

"You can't leave," Madison cried.

"If you leave, I'm going with you." Fitz waved goodbye.

She's leaving. Ben had the urge to do a little two-step. He didn't feel bad for making her leave. It was the only solution. His crew would be upset for a day or two, then things would return to normal and—

"I know about the bet."

It was so quiet you could have heard a transponder ping three miles underwater. No one moved. No one even blinked.

Ben stared at Kayla, unsure where her announcement fell in with her goodbyes.

"I'm flattered. Truly flattered, but marriage..." She flipped her hair behind her shoulder, and Ben's groin tightened. No doubt she didn't have a clue how sexy that move was or she wouldn't have done it just then. Poor guys. He hoped they knew she wasn't torturing them on purpose. "It's not for me."

"Ever?" Anguish filled Eugene's voice.

"Not right now." Her bottom lip quivered slightly. "Or in the near future, either."

"But in the not-so-near future?" Stevie asked.

"I, uh, don't know."

That seemed to give the men hope. They were a pack of rats clinging to lifelines in the middle of a hurricane. It was time to let go and face their fates.

"What about a boyfriend?" Fitz's constant smile was nowhere in sight. "Are you looking for a boyfriend?"

"The only thing I want to find is the *Isabella*."

Ben heard a collective sigh. He wondered how they would react to her final goodbye. Man, he hoped they didn't cry.

"What about after we find the *Isabella*?" Zach asked.

Ben snickered. Until Kayla stepped aboard, everyone had called the *Isabella* the *Izzy*.

Kayla furrowed her brow. "Do you think mixing business with pleasure is a good idea?"

"Yes," six voices answered without a hesitation of doubt.

She sighed. "Well it doesn't matter, because I could never be interested in a man who made me part of a bet."

Kayla had guts. Nerve, too. Ben respected that. He only wished she'd get on with it and say she was leaving.

"Does this mean you're not interested in any of us?" Monk seemed to be having a hard time comprehending this. "In me?"

"You guys are all great," she said. "And attractive, too."

Monk grinned. "Some more than others."

Kayla's laughter reached across the dining room, and Ben felt as if he'd been hit in the solar plexus. "Each of you has your own special quality."

"What quality?" Zach asked.

"I want to know mine," Stevie said.

Eugene readied his pen. "Me, too."

"You really want to know?" Kayla asked.

Another resounding yes filled the air.

"Well, let's see." She looked to her right. "Stevie has great hair and is the most amazing cook. I need to start working out or my waistline is going to disappear."

Stevie blushed. "That would never happen."

"You are too sweet." Kayla looked at Fitz. "And you have the best sense of humor. I've never laughed or smiled so much in my life."

Fitz made a grand gesture of thanks and fell out of his chair.

"And Zach." Kayla grinned. "This may be a little personal, but you have the nicest butt. So great I wish we didn't have to sit down during our shift so much."

Zach nearly floated off his chair. "Gee, thanks, Kayla."

Fitz smacked Zach on the arm. "She's still not going to marry you."

"And Wolf." The sincerity in Kayla's eyes made Ben sit up and take notice. "I've never met a man so strong, yet so sensitive. Some woman will thank her lucky stars when she lands such a great husband and father."

Wolf sat straighter, and he hugged Madison.

"Eugene." Kayla's smile softened. "How did one man get to be so smart and so cute at the same time?"

"When you combine DNA from—"

"It was a rhetorical question, Einstein," Monk said.

"And Monk." She blew out a puff of air. "You have so much charm it should be illegal. You should be in the movies. Or consider going into politics."

Monk smiled. "Only if you'll be my first lady."

"What about Gray and Vance?" Eugene asked, his pen ready.

"Gray has a killer smile. Those dimples of his are lethal weapons. And Vance is a natural athlete with a great body."

Eugene frowned. "Yes, we know that about Vance."

"Hey, guys." Fitz grinned. "Together we're Kayla's perfect man."

"What about the boss?" Eugene asked.

A deer caught in the headlights had never looked so cute. She bit her bottom lip. "He, uh, wasn't part of the bet."

Ben had to give her credit. She was fast on her feet.

"Come on," Stevie urged. "Tell us."

She tucked a strand of hair behind her ear. "Ben is…nice when he wants to be."

Fitz laughed. "You know what they say about nice guys…"

Everyone laughed. Not Ben. He was nice? The other guys had great butts, smiles, bodies, brains. And he was…nice?

"So you guys aren't mad at me?" Kayla asked.

"No."

"Of course not."

"Disappointed, but not mad."

The men tumbled over themselves to reassure Kayla. Ben didn't care. All he could focus on was *nice*.

Kayla seemed relieved. "And the bet…"

"Off," Wolf said. "I'll return the money."

"Great." The edges of her mouth curled up. "Now I get to stay."

Not stay, say goodbye. Ben wasn't nice. If she'd thought a meaningless compliment would change things, she had another thing coming. He stood. "You're leaving."

Her smiled widened. "I'm staying."

"But we agreed—"

"Yes, we did," she interrupted. "I agreed to leave if we couldn't resolve the problem with the crew. But I resolved it, so I'm staying."

Madison clapped. "She's staying. She's staying."

The crew and Kayla joined in.

"Come on, Daddy," Madison said. "Clap."

Ben gave an unenthusiastic clap and slumped in his chair. A damn mutiny—that's what this was.

Chapter Six

Everything had changed, yet nothing had changed.

Ben had kept his word and moved the search to her coordinates. Transducers were dropped overboard for reference points. Echo sounders helped the crew draw a seabed profile of the newly mapped-out search area. And the first pass was completed.

Sitting in the control room, Kayla stared at the monitors in front of her. Acoustic echoes received by the transducers became electronic impulses that traveled up the cable and into the bank of computers in the control room. Line-by-line images formed on the screens. But there was one problem. The only thing she saw was mud. No debris trails, no interesting geological formation. Nothing but mud.

She glanced at the row of recorders—glorified typewriters and printers—covered in black dust. The whole area smelled like graphite. But no marks were being made to signal a target or anomaly standing out from all the sediment.

The ship was now on its second line, making its way back at a constant two knots, slightly overlapping the previous pass. They called it mowing the lawn. It was more like watching the grass grow. Kayla sighed.

What was happening to her? She hadn't felt this restless before. But the success or failure of the search rested on her shoulders. She could no longer blame Ben for looking in the wrong place. And the longer it took to find the ship, the antsier she got.

The *Isabella* was out there. Where?

The investors and the museum were counting on her. Her reputation was on the line. And her father…

She touched the talisman around her neck. The indentations beneath the pads of her fingertips were like old friends. She could describe the talisman by memory—pie-shaped and two inches long with untranslatable markings.

She had to find the *Isabella*. Not only for everyone else, but for herself, too. Her father's research had given her a clue about her past. Symbols written alongside his notes about the lost pirate ship matched those on her necklace—an heirloom from her mother's family. If she found the ship, maybe she could find answers about her past. The odds were unbelievable. Kayla didn't care. She was alone and tired of living a life punctuated with question marks.

Kayla stared at the monitors and forced herself to stay awake. She yawned and stretched her arms above her head. Her body clock still hadn't adjusted to this shift. She wondered if it ever would.

"Coffee?"

"No, thanks." Kayla glanced back, surprised to see Ben at this time of night.

He wore gray sweatpants and a white T-shirt and

looked as if he'd just rolled out of bed. A day's growth of whiskers made him look more dangerous and even a little sexy. He brushed his hand through his sleep-rumpled hair. The careless style looked good on him. Too good for a man she wanted to avoid at all costs.

Their relationship had worsened since the other night when she'd confronted the crew about the bet. She still couldn't believe she'd pulled that off. A good portion of her success she owed to Ben. Indirectly, of course. He made her reach inside herself and do things she'd never thought possible. She'd tried to emulate Ben's strengths, be bold and daring. It had given her the courage to take a stand.

Everyone seemed to respect what she'd done. Everyone except Ben. The tension between them had increased to the point where even Madison noticed.

"What's going on?" he asked.

"Nothing." She wished he would go back to his cabin. "Aren't you supposed to be asleep?"

"I was, but Madison woke up. Baby Fifi fell out of bed and she wanted a glass of water."

"Doesn't Baby Fifi drink from a bottle?"

His easy, sleepy smile, the first directed her way in days, was as warm and comfy as a pair of flannel jammies.

He glanced around. "Where's Zach?"

"He traded shifts with Monk tonight."

"So where's Monk?"

She pointed to the monitor showing Monk as he checked the cable on the big drum. "On deck."

Any trace of sleepiness disappeared. Ben was alert and ready. For what, she didn't know. "You shouldn't be alone."

"Monk will be right back. I know what to do if a target shows up."

"Did something break?"

"Monk wanted to check the cable." Ben's eyes darkened. He apparently didn't believe her. "That's all I know," she said.

He raised a brow. "A little defensive."

"If I looked at you as if you'd stolen the last cookie in the jar, you'd be a little defensive, too." The firm set of his chin told her not to expect an apology, but she wanted to understand him better. If only to avoid future confrontations. "Are you like this with everyone? Or just me?"

"A combination."

Figures. Kayla shouldn't have asked in the first place, but Ben brought out both the best and the worst in her. She wasn't normally so in-your-face. She was quiet and boring. Like her father, she preferred the company of books, charts and old journals to people. Maybe too much of Ben was rubbing off on her. Or perhaps something about him rubbed her the wrong way. His swagger, his self-assuredness, his arrogance? It could be a number of things. She studied the monitor. More mud.

"You didn't play fair," Ben said finally.

"I played by the rules you set."

"What rules?"

"Exactly." She glanced at him, his eyes sharp and assessing. "I've said it before. This isn't about you or me. The *Isabella* is bigger than both of us. Bigger than ego and pride."

He didn't reply and she didn't care.

"I don't understand why you're so upset," she admitted. "You finished your search. Examined the targets. It was time to move on."

"We could have expanded the search area."

"Again?" She caught his glare in the reflection of one of the digital displays. "The *Isabella* is here." She sounded more confident than she felt, but her research was correct. It had to be. "She's here."

"Is that your instinct or your psychic talking?"

"It's the research."

"Ah, yes." He sat in the chair next to her and studied the monitors. "Your brilliant research that reads more like a novel with swashbuckling pirates, forbidden love and mermaids."

His words stung, but she understood. She hadn't shared any of her research with him, but he wasn't alone. Not even the museum knew how much she'd discovered about the *Isabella*.

The recorders sparked to life. Kayla jumped out of her chair and ran. An image was being drawn on the paper. "Sonar action. Lots of sonar action."

"Talk to me," Ben said.

"Contact off port 120 meters." She called out targets while she wrote the time of contact in the margin of the strip chart and in the logbook. Ben radioed the bridge, asking for the ship's speed and position. The altitude of the sled, the gain on the signal, the length of towline all had to be recorded, too. Stuff happened so fast, Kayla didn't have time to blink.

"Monk, get in here," Ben yelled into the walkie-talkie. "Now."

Kayla called out more targets and noted the times on the strip chart. If they didn't get all the information, it would be difficult if not impossible to find the target again. Her fingers cramped from writing so fast, but she didn't stop.

Monk burst into the control room. "Do you see what I see, boss?"

Kayla knew Monk wouldn't tell her what he saw. Ben had an important rule in the control room. No one could say out loud what was seen on the screen. That way no one person's perception influenced another's. Everything was written down and compared later.

"Major action. Contact 150 meters port." Kayla stared at the recorders. Adrenaline rushed through her veins. "Something big is out there. We're talking big."

The *Isabella?* Was it the *Isabella?*

Kayla's heart pounded. She could barely breathe.

"Be ready to take this thing up, Monk," Ben said. "We don't want to hit anything."

She couldn't believe how calm he sounded. The man had nerves of steel. She was sweating, and it was less than sixty-eight degrees in here. Kayla unzipped her jacket.

Monk sat at the controls. "I'm ready, boss."

"Get it up now," Ben ordered.

Kayla saw something. A ridge. An outcropping of rock in the sediment. No, it wasn't geological. It was…a ship.

The *Isabella.*

She knew it had to be the ship. Excitement coursed through her. She enjoyed the moment for about two seconds and went back to work recording information.

"We're past it." Her voice sounded much calmer than she felt. But the work continued. Gathering all the information, recording it in the logbook, breathing again. Finally, they finished.

Monk yelped. He grabbed Kayla and gave her a quick hug. "You did it, darlin'."

"We did do it." She felt like such a member of a

team, one of the crew. For once, she belonged, and
Kayla loved the feeling. They had worked so well together, even she and Ben.

He shook Monk's hand and walked over to Kayla.
"Good job."

"Thanks." Her cheeks warmed. Ben's compliment
meant more than it should, but she was too happy to
worry about that now. "You weren't so bad yourself."

Kayla hugged him. An impulsive gesture, as Monk's
had been to her. She didn't expect a hug back. But she
got one. A good one.

Ben pulled her closer, enveloping her in his warmth.
His soap-and-water scent was an intoxicating elixir.
Blood roared through her veins. Her temperature soared.
She didn't want to let go of Ben so she didn't.

She relished being in his arms. A warm glow flowed
through her. Kayla felt as if she'd come home. And it
was a place she didn't want to leave. Not anytime soon.

Was he feeling the same thing? She didn't want to
know.

Kayla waited for him to let go of her.

But he didn't.

Her heart hammered against her chest, against his. The
intensity of attraction surprised her.

Attraction?

They didn't get along. It couldn't be attraction.

Yet he continued holding her. And she still liked it.

But this wasn't right. No matter how wonderful hug-
ging him felt, it wasn't the right time for either one of
them.

Kayla pulled away, but Ben held on to her. A rush of
power raced through her. She'd never felt so feminine
and strong. She wanted him to find her desirable. She'd
never cared about that in the past, but with Ben…

She pulled away again. This time he released her.

"I know what I saw." Monk brought up targets on the monitors. He filtered images and magnified them. The colors on the screen changed. "We all saw the same thing."

"But is it the right one?" Ben asked.

It had to be the right one. Kayla glanced at his profile, silhouetted against the glow from the monitors, and sucked in a breath. He looked more like a pirate than ever. Dark, dangerous, desirable. Tingly sensations raced along her nerve endings. From the top of her head all the way to her toes.

She should be paying attention to what Monk was doing, but she couldn't stop staring at Ben. She didn't want to look away. It was as if she were seeing him for the first time, which made zero sense. She'd seen him plenty of times before, but each time his pull was stronger. This time more than the rest combined.

"It's the right one." Monk typed on the keyboard and measured the images. "Come on."

The impatience in his voice was enough to get her focused. Kayla studied the monitor and bit her lip. The *Isabella* was her priority. Not Ben.

"Damn. It's long." Monk continued typing. Another image appeared on the screen. A cylinder. Most likely an exhaust stack.

Kayla's heart sank to her feet. She wouldn't be surprised if her heart kept going until it hit the ocean floor and buried itself in the mud.

It wasn't the *Isabella*.

Monk cursed. She'd never heard some of the words spewing from his mouth. "Sorry, Kayla," he said after his tirade.

"It's okay." She forced the words from her dry throat.

She understood what Monk was feeling. Total devastation. Kayla slumped into a chair.

A vein on Ben's neck throbbed. He pressed his lips together and squeezed her shoulder. "This happens all the time."

Knowing that tidbit of information didn't make her feel better. Her emotions had gone from an all-time high to lower than low. She wanted to look away from the monitor so the exhaust stack would stop taunting her, but she couldn't. The image hypnotized her. It wasn't supposed to be turning out this way. It wasn't supposed to be this difficult. "I thought we'd find the *Isabella* on the first pass."

Ben removed his hand, and a part of her wished he was still touching her. "Do you know the odds—"

"Anything's possible."

"Let me guess," he said. "You buy lotto tickets?"

"Not funny."

"I'm sorry, Kayla." His voice softened when he said her name, and she felt a little catch inside. He turned her chair away from the monitor so she couldn't see it. "The *Izzy* is out there. We didn't find her tonight, but we will."

Conviction laced each of his words. He smiled, and she felt a tiny bit better. Enough to smile back. "I do buy lotto tickets if the jackpot gets really big."

"Knew it."

"You?"

"Never." His gaze held hers. "My dad's spent too much money trying to hit the big one. He's been searching for the pot of gold at the end of the rainbow for as long as I can remember."

"Is he a treasure hunter?"

"He wants to be a treasure finder. He's always been

a big dreamer, but things never progress past the dream stage once he realizes how much work is involved.''

''Does he come out on jobs with you?''

''No. He'd rather follow a rumor or wait for a hot tip and let instinct lead him to the buried treasure.''

Things were starting to make sense to Kayla. But she wanted—no, needed—to know more. ''What about your mom?''

''She's wonderful.'' Ben's smile spoke volumes about his love for his mother. ''She supports my dad's get-rich-quick schemes. Spoils Madison and me rotten. And holds everything together. She deserves…so much more.''

This was the most open he'd been with Kayla. And she liked it. A lot. ''After we find the *Isabella*, you can give her all she deserves.''

He nodded. ''It's been a busy night. We're almost at the end of the line. It'll take hours to turn the ship around and start on the next pass. There won't be anything for you to see. Why don't you get some sleep?''

''Okay.''

Ben looked surprised she'd agreed with him.

Kayla didn't know whether it was his hug or his belief in finding the *Isabella* or hearing about his father, but Ben had made her feel better. They had started out on the wrong foot, and it was worth a second try. She would make things right between them.

''See you later,'' he said.

She smiled. ''You can count on it.''

Counting sheep hadn't worked. Neither had reading a publication from UNESCO on international salvage rights. Alcohol wasn't allowed on board except for a couple of bottles of celebratory champagne, so a shot of whiskey was out of the question.

Ben lay in his bed. Physically, he was tired. Mentally, he couldn't shut off his brain. He couldn't stop thinking about Kayla. The way she'd handled the pressure in the control room, the way she'd felt in his arms.

So soft, so warm, so perfect.

One whiff of her citrus-smelling hair and he'd been a goner. Not even Monk's presence had made Ben end the hug when he should have. But holding Kayla's body in his arms had felt so good. He hadn't wanted to let go.

Somehow he'd controlled his impulses, dammed up the testosterone, kept the blood from rushing to places he didn't want it to go. But now he was paying the price.

He wanted to touch her. Kiss her.

More than that, Ben wanted an explanation. A reason for what he was feeling. Yes, she was gorgeous. But he'd been around beautiful women before. He'd married and divorced one. His attraction to Kayla made no sense; his attraction to her broke every rule.

Kayla Waterton was here not only as a representative of the museum and investors, but as a member of his crew. He couldn't think of her as anything but one of the guys. But he wasn't doing that.

Hell, he'd told her about his father. Ben never opened up like that, but the look of disappointment on her face when she saw the exhaust stack had nearly ripped out his heart. He'd needed something, anything to take her mind off the wreck not being the *Izzy*. He'd punted. And scored.

But at what cost?

Even if the situation were different, his life wasn't. Ben only had room for two women in his life: Madison and the sea.

* * *

Kayla couldn't sleep. Her brain wouldn't turn off. Not with so much on her mind. The *Isabella* and Ben. She wasn't sure where one started and the other ended. But she'd come to a decision. She wanted to show Ben her research, and she didn't want to wait until morning. With her satchel in hand, Kayla knocked on Ben's cabin door.

The door cracked opened. Ben's eyes widened. She'd surprised him twice in one night. That had to be a record. Kayla smiled. "I hope I didn't wake you."

"I couldn't sleep."

"Me, neither." She shifted from foot to foot. "May I come in?"

He opened the door farther. As she stepped inside, Kayla was more aware of his surroundings than the first time she'd been here. She loved all of Madison's artwork decorating the walls. The photographs of her and the crew. This wasn't a cabin on a ship but a home, and all of it spoke volumes about Ben Mendoza.

"What's wrong?" he asked.

"Nothing's wrong. It's just…" She opened her satchel and removed the copy of her research on the *Isabella*. The original was stored at home in a safe. "I wanted you to see this."

He took the five-inch stack of paper. "What is it?"

Her palms were sweating. She hadn't been this nervous since her first date when Tony Bauer wanted to park up on Council Crest—otherwise known as make-out central. "My research."

"On the *Izzy?*"

"Yes."

His eyes gleamed with interest. "Why?"

Good question. Kayla wasn't sure herself. Maybe she wanted to show him he wasn't chasing a pipe dream like his father had so many times. Maybe she liked being part of the crew tonight and didn't want it to end. Maybe she wanted to share a piece of herself with him. Maybe she needed someone to tell her she was right.

She smiled. "It's time."

Chapter Seven

Sunlight streamed through the porthole. Ben had sat in the same chair and read all night, but he wasn't tired. He didn't want to stop until he'd read every page.

This was it. Kayla did know what she was talking about.

He'd been a stubborn idiot for not giving her more credit. Hell, any credit. She might be a dreamer, but there was more to her than he originally thought. She'd used everything from the Spanish archives to a journal from an eighteenth-century astronomer to research the *Izzy*.

He glanced over at his bed. She was sound asleep, curled up on her side facing him. Her chest rose with her even breaths and the corners of her mouth tipped up in a serene smile. Her hair spread out over his pillowcase. The image was as sexy as he imagined it would be. He was tempted to crawl into bed with her, to put his arms around her warm body and pull her close.

But he couldn't.

He rose, covered Kayla with a blanket and sat back in his chair. She didn't stir. He wanted to keep reading, but he also wanted to look at Kayla.

She blinked open her eyes. "Wh-where am I?"

"In my cabin."

Kayla bolted upright. "In your bed?"

"Yes."

"I fell asleep." She stared at him. "And you had to sleep in the chair. I'm so sorry."

"I didn't sleep, so don't feel bad." He motioned to the papers on his lap. "I've been reading your research."

Anticipation filled her eyes. Ben waited. She leaned toward him. Any farther and she'd fall off the bed.

"And?" she asked finally.

"It's…brilliant."

She started to speak. No doubt, to contradict him. And then she furrowed her brow. "You think?"

"I think."

Tension evaporated from her face. She tilted her chin, but her eyes reflected her gratitude. "I told you so."

"Yes, you did." He laughed. "You love what you do."

"Why do you say that?"

He patted her research. "I read your work. Your passion leaps off the page."

"Thanks." Her wistful smile touched his heart. "I love my job. It's like being a detective and trying to solve a mystery from the past. When all the clues and pieces come together—" Kayla sighed "—there's nothing like it."

His gaze met hers. Neither spoke, but the silence was surprisingly comfortable. At least for him.

She pushed away the blanket and hopped off his bed. "I should get going."

He didn't want her to leave. But asking her to stay wasn't an option. Saying goodbye was the smartest thing he could do. Ben rose. "Can I keep this until I finish reading it?"

"Yes." She couldn't get to the door fast enough.

"Thanks."

An edge of her mouth curved. "You're welcome."

What was going on? This exchange was too polite. Too forced. Ben didn't like it. He didn't want to be acting this way with Kayla. They'd finally moved forward and he didn't want to take any backward steps.

She reached for the door handle.

"Wait." The word escaped before he had time to think. He wasn't sure what he wanted from Kayla but knew he didn't want her to leave.

She faced him, a questioning look in her eyes. His gaze dropped to her mouth. One taste. That's all he wanted. She parted her lips to speak, but Ben didn't give her a chance. He covered her mouth with his.

Impulsive, yes. Insane, definitely.

But he didn't care.

He didn't care about anything except kissing Kayla. He'd care later, but not now. Not when she felt so perfect in his arms. His kiss was light, gentle, controlled.

It wasn't enough. It would never be enough.

But any more was out of the question.

He settled for what he could have and drank in her sweetness.

Kayla leaned into him and deepened the kiss with an urgency all her own. Her hunger surprised him, intrigued him, excited him. As her hands splayed across his back, he pulled her closer. Her soft breasts pressed against his chest, and his blood burned. Forget about finding a lost treasure of gold and silver and jewels. He was holding a living, breathing treasure in his arms. This was what he'd been searching for, what had been missing from his life.

It was only a kiss.

Yeah, right. Only a kiss that left him feeling invincible, as if he could conquer land and sea.

He wound his fingers in her hair, the strands as silky as he imagined. A soft moan escaped from her lips.

His control slipped a notch. And another. He drew the kiss to an end before he lost it completely. Ben stepped back.

Her eyes wide, Kayla stared up at him. A faint blush tinged her cheeks.

Silence stretched between them. Ben didn't like it. "I'm—"

"If you say you're sorry, I'm going to hit you."

Her reaction amused him, but Ben knew better than to smile. He was going to apologize, but not for that. He might have opened a can of sardines and added a boatload of complications to his life and the expedition, but he wasn't sorry for kissing her. "I should have asked you first."

"Asked me?"

"Asked permission to kiss you."

"I would have said no."

"Then it's good I didn't ask." He was too much a gentleman to remind her of her reaction to the kiss. The hell he was. He lounged against the doorway. "Why did you kiss me back if you didn't want me to kiss you in the first place?"

Her bottom lip quivered. "I—I have to go."

She reached for the door handle again. This time he didn't stop her.

"Thanks," he said. "For…everything."

She nodded. He wanted her to say something. She didn't.

"See you later?" he asked.

Another nod. Not the response he wanted, but it would have to do. For now.

"You're up early."

The sound of Wolf's voice made Kayla look up. The big man was walking toward her, and she hadn't noticed him. She took her fingertips off her lips. Lips swollen and tingling from Ben's kiss. All she could think about was getting back to her cabin and processing what had happened.

"Yes." Her mind reeled. A coherent conversation was not possible. What had she done? Ben had complimented her research and he'd kissed her. She wasn't sure which she liked better, which one she needed more.

"You okay?" Concern filled Wolf's voice.

She wasn't okay. She didn't know if she would ever be okay again. Soft, gentle, caring. Ben's tenderness had surprised Kayla. A caress with his lips was how his kiss had felt. But she hadn't let it remain that way. No, a brush of his lips hadn't been enough for her. She had thrown herself at him. And enjoyed it.

Why had she told Ben she would have said no? That only made it worse after the way she'd reacted to his kiss. Was it possible to die from embarrassment?

"Kayla?"

"Long night."

"I know how that goes."

In this instance, she didn't think Wolf did.

"Get some sleep."

"Okay," she muttered.

Kayla sidestepped Wolf, continued walking to her

cabin as if on autopilot, and opened the door. Inside, her hand shook as she closed the door and clicked the lock into place. She would get through this. Somehow things would turn out fine.

It was only a kiss. A nice kiss. A nice, shatter-her-view-of-the-universe kind of kiss.

The memory made her knees wobble. She slid to the floor.

Her need for him shocked her. Then and now.

Her heart pounded, her pulse raced, and her stomach did half-gainers with quarter-twists. Goose bumps covered her skin, but she felt warm.

Oh, no. She nearly smacked her forehead.

All the weird feelings she'd experienced—the aches and pains, the itching and shivering. It wasn't an allergy or injury; it was Ben. Her attraction to him was manifesting itself in physical symptoms.

One mystery solved.

But that didn't make her feel better.

Kayla still had a problem. A big problem. And his name was Ben Mendoza.

"It's not worth a second look." Vance's nostrils flared. "We'd be wasting our time. What do you think, Kayla?"

"I'm not an expert." Earlier she'd studied the strip charts from yesterday's sonar scans, but she had another job at the moment—sitting on the lounge floor and coloring with Madison in her Little Mermaid book. "But it looks geological."

"Thank you." Vance smiled. "Take another look, Gray. See how it's rounded. That's geological. No question."

This target discussion between Vance and Gray had

been going on all day and intensified by the hour. Finding no other targets hadn't helped. The *Isabella* was out there. Kayla kept telling herself that. It was only a matter of time before the ship appeared on one of the sonar scans. They would break open the bubbly and celebrate. She picked up a purple crayon and colored Ariel's tail.

Gray massaged his temples. "After a couple hundred years on the bottom of the ocean, a target isn't going to look like a ship. It would be rounded. Amorphous."

Madison held her pink crayon in the air. "What's 'amorsus'?"

"Amorphous," Gray repeated with that great dimpled smile of his. "It means formless. It has no shape."

"Okay." Madison colored a seahorse pink.

Vance wasn't swayed. "It's geological and not worth a second look."

"They argue a lot, don't they?" Madison whispered.

"Vance and Gray aren't arguing," Kayla said. "They're having a discussion."

"What's going on?" Ben asked. "I can hear you all the way on the bridge."

What was he doing here? Being underfoot was one thing. This bordered on the ridiculous. No matter how hard Kayla tried, she couldn't avoid him. At least they weren't alone. She didn't want to discuss the kiss they'd shared yesterday.

"We're coloring, and Vance and Gray are talking, Daddy," Madison said. "About the *Issy*."

"*Izzy,*" Ben corrected her. "Don't tell me you're still discussing the target?"

Vance winked. "Okay, boss, we won't tell you."

"I read more of your research, Kayla." Ben's smile irritated her. She preferred his frown—make that his scowl. "It's incredible."

This was how he'd been since yesterday. Complimenting her, being helpful, making her laugh. He was a pirate, not a cruise director or self-improvement guru. It was much easier to dislike him when he acted like an arrogant jerk.

Kayla wanted to forget about kissing him, but every time she saw him the memories rushed back. He was too handsome, too sexy. But he wasn't nice. If Ben were a nice man, he would keep his distance and leave her alone. But he hadn't. Definitely not nice.

"Hop up, princess," he said to Madison. She didn't hesitate. She dropped her crayon, grabbed Baby Fifi and climbed on Ben's lap. He tickled her.

She giggled. "Is there room for Kayla?"

Mischief flashed in Ben's eyes. Kayla glanced at Gray and Vance, who still argued about the target. "I—I'm fine here."

"The floor's uncomfortable." Ben's smile widened. "We can make room."

His charming grin unleashed a bevy of butterflies in her stomach. She gripped the crayon so hard it snapped. "Thanks, but I'm coloring."

Kayla concentrated on the tiny seashells coming to life on the page with each stroke of her crayon. Not bad. She wouldn't be giving the artist Wyland any competition, but she was pleased. Maybe she should take art lessons when she got home.

Madison giggled again. Kayla glanced up and her breath caught in her throat. Father and daughter shared a precious moment together. Smiling, laughing, cuddling. Kayla's heart filled with joy. Their love was so strong she could almost touch it. He was the kind of father she wanted for her children.

Her children.

Kayla's quickening pulse sent off a warning. The lines of the picture in the coloring book blurred. What was happening to her? Imagining a family, let alone a future with Ben, was out of the question. She wanted to avoid him, not fantasize or dream about him.

But whatever she felt was turning into something more. She knew that as well as she knew her own name. Her feelings for Ben grew each time they interacted, whether alone or not. But she couldn't be alone with him. Not ever again. He would want to talk to her about what had happened in his cabin. The last thing she wanted to do was talk. And that didn't leave any other options except kissing. And she sure couldn't kiss him again. No matter how much she might want to.

As a million stars twinkled against the night sky, the almost-full moon cast its glow on the waves. A breeze ruffled the ends of Kayla's hair. She stood at the rail alone. Finally…

For the past two days, Ben had wanted a chance to be alone with her. Until now, it hadn't happened. She was always with someone—one of the crew or Madison. If he didn't know better, he would think Kayla was avoiding him. Great. Now he was becoming paranoid. "Mind if I join you?"

She didn't look at him. "Go ahead."

Not the most enthusiastic invitation, but he would take it. He stood next to her and held on to the railing. Ben hoped Kayla realized he wasn't interested in a repeat performance of the other morning. Much as he would like more kisses, it wasn't a smart idea. And he had to be smart about this. He couldn't make a mistake, or worse, fail.

But he wanted to know her better, to figure out how

she'd managed to crawl under his skin, to know why she'd become important to him. They hadn't gotten along well. They were so different. Why would he want her? Lust? It couldn't be that simple.

But nothing else explained his impulsive and selfish behavior. Behavior that had to stop. Not tomorrow. Not tonight. But now. The *Izzy* was waiting to be discovered, but the only thing on his mind was Kayla.

Ben had to do something about her. His first choice would be to hide away in his cabin with her and ravish each other until they were out of each other's systems, but that wasn't an option. That left talking. Communication had never been one of his strong points, as his ex-wife would agree, but what choice did he have?

A shooting star streaked through the sky. Ben wasn't sure how to start. Might as well dive in. "It's a beautiful night."

She nodded. "I saw a school of dolphins swim by."

"Did they say hello?"

"No, they just waved." As she stared at the water, she scratched her leg. "It's weird. I've been feeling as if nothing exists except this ship and all of us on board."

"That's what happens when you're out at sea for any length of time. Life on the ship becomes a world unto itself. I worry about Madison because of that. Not now, but when she's older."

"You don't want to continue with your salvage operation?"

"I don't know." He'd had these concerns for more than a year now but had never voiced them. Something about Kayla made it easy to open up. It was strange. "I always figured I would do the exact opposite of my father and stick to one thing my entire life. Be career navy.

Work hard, travel and retire with a pension." Ben shrugged. "Didn't happen."

Kayla's interested gaze met his. "Why?"

If only the answer was as simple as the question. "Some wet-behind-the-ears officer wanted glory at any cost. He forgot about the need to know policy. And in this case, it was info we needed to know."

"Was that how you got hurt?"

Ben nodded. "It was supposed to be a simple recovery operation, but we didn't have a clue what we were getting ourselves into. There was an explosion. The entire hull blew." Ben remembered getting trapped inside, trying to reach his buddies, being dragged out and reaching the surface when he was sure he would drown inside the twisted steel death trap. "I decided if I was going to die, I'd be the one with the knowledge and making the life-or-death choices. So I left once my time was up."

"And you ended up here?" she asked.

"It took a few years. I worked with various salvage operators. Did some cargo recovery, demolition work— you name it—anything underwater. Always wanted my own operation but couldn't afford it."

"Until the *Santa Theresa.*"

He raised a brow.

"I did my research," she admitted. "Your design of the GOTCHA ROV made that expedition a success. Why do you think the museum was so happy to have you on the team?"

He grinned. "My good looks."

"You didn't send a picture with your résumé."

"Should I have?" Ben didn't expect an answer. Her smile was enough. "Once we settled the lawsuits and determined our ownership of the gold and artifacts from the *St. T*, I had enough to start my own salvage operation."

"Xmarks Explorers?"

"X marks the spot and we explore."

"Very clever."

"Go on."

Her laughter bubbled over and surrounded his heart. He really had to put a stop to this. "I figured I'd be a salvor forever. And then Madison came along. Now only time will tell." Ben was doing all the talking. Kayla's turn to open up. "What about you?"

"Me?"

He rested his elbows on the railing. "What do you see in your future?"

"Finding the *Isabella*."

"After that?"

"I don't know." She stared at the water, a faraway look in her eyes. "I've got the museum and my research. I teach at a local university and would love to start a cooperative program between them."

"What about a family?" Ben wasn't sure why he asked the question or why he wanted to know the answer so badly.

"My only goal is to find the *Isabella*."

"Seriously?"

She nodded. "I need to find some answers."

"Answers?"

"It—it's nothing." She rubbed her fingers on her necklace. "Just some stuff."

Stuff? Ben didn't buy it. He'd gotten good at reading people. Kayla was holding back, but he wouldn't push her. Not yet.

"What's around your neck?" he asked.

"A necklace. It belonged to my mother's family."

He noticed strange writings on it. "What does it say?"

"The markings can't be translated or identified. I've tried. Not one linguist or ancient-language expert has a clue."

"Can I see it?" Ben asked.

She nodded.

As he reached for the necklace, his hand brushed her. The slight contact was enough to affect his heart rate. He ignored it. "Silver?"

"I think so, but it doesn't tarnish."

"Interesting." He turned the talisman over. Her warm breath caressed his hand. It felt much too good. He released the necklace. "Did your father tell you anything about it?"

"From the time I was little, he told me how important it was. He said I'd learn a big secret on my sixteenth birthday, but..."

"He never got the chance to tell you."

"No." Her mouth tightened. "They told me about the accident in the submersible. They said he never knew what happened, never felt any pain. At that depth, the pressure...he didn't stand a chance. But I didn't believe them."

"Submersible? Your father..." Ben remembered the accident but had never made the connection until now. He gazed into her eyes. "Your father was Jason Waterton."

She nodded. "The sea took both my mother and my father."

"Oh, Kayla." Ben wanted to comfort her, to hold her, but a touch would have to do. He covered her hand with his. "I...I don't know what to say."

"No one does. Not even me. I thought it was all a

mistake. He was one of the leading shipwreck historians
in the world. He knew everything about the ocean. How
a ship might sink, where it would settle on the bottom,
everything. His percentage of finds was astronomical.
How could this have happened to him? I kept waiting
for him to come home. But he never did. He was gone.
And I was alone.'' She pulled her hand away. ''Still am
alone.''

''You're not alone.''

She glanced down at the water. Dark, unfathomable,
unforgiving. ''Yes, I am.''

Ben raised her chin with his fingertips. The hurt in
her eyes hit him full force. ''What about us?''

''Us?''

''Me, Madison, Wolf, Monk, the rest of the crew.''
Ben wanted to help. He wanted to wipe away the tears
and make her feel safe and secure, but he didn't know
how and felt out of his element. ''We might not be the
prettiest bunch of characters, you and Madison excluded,
but you're one of us. One of the crew.''

Her eyes glimmered. With happy tears? he wondered
and hoped. ''Me?'' she asked.

Ben heard the hope resting with that one word. He
didn't know how to answer. Not when he couldn't believe he'd spoken those words in the first place. The
beginnings of a smile appeared on her face. This was
important to her, more than he possibly realized. Any
regrets he may have had about including her with his
ragtag crew disappeared.

''Think about it.'' Ben liked how her gaze never left
his. ''You fit in better than anyone expected. You've
contributed more than anyone thought.''

She was intelligent, caring, strong...and a hell of a lot
prettier than anyone had imagined.

The corners of her mouth tipped upward. "You make it sound as if you thought I'd only take up space."

"And eat food." A satisfied smile formed on his lips. "Admit it, you didn't have a high opinion of any of us when you stepped on board."

"Only because—"

"We were looking in the wrong place."

"Do you blame me?"

Not for that. But she was one-hundred-percent responsible for the tingling feeling in the pit of his stomach. Ben didn't get it. He never tingled. "Let's put it behind us. The past is the past. No sense dredging it up again."

"Does that mean putting, uh, everything behind us?"

Ben stared at her. "You mean the, uh, what happened the other morning?"

She nodded.

He was getting an out, a free pass. He'd be stupid not to take it. "Yes. Kissing members of the crew is against the rules. We've got a lot to do and I don't want any of my crew to be distracted."

"By your kisses?"

He laughed.

She pursed her lips. "Any other rules?"

"I treat all members of my crew the same, so don't expect any special treatment."

"I wouldn't want it any other way," she said. "I just want to be one of the guys."

"No problem." Easier said than done, he realized once the words were out.

"Thanks." Kayla smiled. "You're very sweet, boss."

Ben looped his thumb in his belt loop. Being called "sweet" ranked up there with "nice." But this time it didn't bother him so much. No, he was more concerned with her calling him "boss."

Chapter Eight

The days passed quickly.

Kayla wanted to find the *Isabella,* but a part of her hoped it took a little longer. She couldn't believe she felt this way, but it was true. She loved being part of the crew. Loved the camaraderie. Loved the squabbles over everything from what targets should be reexamined to whether the *Titanic* should be considered a gravesite or not.

She glanced at her watch. Time was meaningless out here with three exceptions—shift times, mealtimes and naptime. "Come on, Madison, time for your nap."

Madison sat at the railing with Baby Fifi on her lap and stared at the water, waiting for the merman to appear. Once again, he'd been a no-show. "Four more minutes."

"One."

"Three."

"Two more." Kayla had learned naptime negotiations from watching Ben. "But that's all."

"Shh." Madison placed her finger on her lips. "Use your quiet voice, please. You'll scare the mermaid boy."

Kayla smiled and rose from her chair. The least she could do was help look for the merman. She searched the water and saw the peaks of the swells. No mermaids. No dolphins. Not even a tanker on the horizon.

Maybe they'd have better luck tomorrow with both the merman and the *Isabella*. Kayla bit her lip. She wasn't ready to leave the people she'd come to care about. The crew, Madison, Ben.

She still couldn't stop thinking about Ben's kiss. Not that it meant anything. The kiss had been an anomaly never to be repeated again.

And that was okay. She wasn't about to ruin her relationship with the other crew members over her strange attraction to Ben Mendoza.

So what if he was a great kisser?

That wasn't important in the grand scheme of things. She finally fit in. That's what mattered. There were plenty of other fish in the sea, but she wasn't ready to drop her hook in the water any time soon. She hadn't been looking to catch one now.

Not that she'd caught Ben.

He wasn't beating a path to her cabin and trying to kiss her again. Sure, he was always around, but he was being friendly and treating her like any other member of his crew. And that's exactly what she wanted. Nothing more.

Everything was fine. The way it should be.

Footsteps sounded. Someone was running. And shouting.

"Die, you pitiful excuse for a human being," a man yelled.

Kayla turned. Water hit her full force. A jet of cold,

really cold, water. Another stream hit her from the other direction. She managed not to scream. Madison screamed loud enough for the both of them.

"I'm sorry." Vance looked sheepish, a high-powered squirt gun in his hands. Water dribbled from the barrel and onto the deck. "We didn't think anyone was around."

Those Super Soakers really worked. Kayla licked her lip. Salty. They must have filled the squirt guns with seawater. At least they hadn't wasted fresh water.

"We usually hear the Little Bit when she's up here." Gray held a matching squirt gun. "Sorry you got caught in the crossfire."

Madison stared at her clothes. "I'm all wet. Baby Fifi is wet."

Kayla was soaked all the way through. Her T-shirt was transparent. Not again. She crossed her arms over her chest. "Me, too."

"What's going on?" someone yelled from below.

"Me and Kayla are all wet," Madison said.

Ben bounded up the steps, followed by Monk, Wolf and Eugene. "What happened?"

"Friendly fire," Kayla explained.

"Are you okay, Madison?" he asked.

"I'm fine, Daddy."

Eugene stared at Kayla, his mouth gaping open. He must have missed the first time this happened. At least Monk and Wolf were subtler. She tried to cover herself better.

Ben noticed his crew's appreciative glances at her current state of wetness and grimaced. "If you're not holding a squirt gun or soaking wet, go back to work."

The three men shuffled down the stairs, mumbling and cursing about the unfairness of life under the command of Captain Bligh. Kayla remembered how she'd questioned his capability to run this expedition. She'd been wrong.

"Thanks," she said.

"They're harmless," Ben said.

Especially with you around. She'd never felt so safe, so secure, as she did with him. Kayla smiled. "I know."

"But these two." He motioned to the guilty shooters. "What do you have to say for yourselves?"

"Sorry, boss," Gray said.

Vance nodded. "Me, too."

"I'm not the one you should be apologizing to," Ben said.

"Sorry," both men mumbled to her and Madison.

"Anything we can do to make it better?" Gray asked.

Madison nodded. "Candy."

"Candy would be nice." Kayla's legs itched again. Must be the saltwater irritating her skin. "And towels."

"Be right back." Gray sprinted away.

Ben stared at Vance. "Don't you have something to do?" As Vance hurried off, Ben handed Kayla a towel. "You okay?"

"I'm fine." He didn't look at her. She might be part of the crew, but with her clothes wet and clinging to her, she was still a female. He hadn't noticed. She uncrossed her arms to scratch her legs again. Kayla figured Ben would at least sneak a peek. He didn't glance her way.

Madison shivered. "I'm cold, Daddy."

He picked her up. "Is that better, princess?"

She nodded. "Now you're wet, too. Can we go swimming in our clothes?"

"Not right now. It's naptime."

"Can Kayla come?"

"She's always welcome to come with us."

Of course she was. Kayla had gotten what she wanted. She was part of the crew. She fit in so well, he didn't realize she was a woman. Just one of the guys.

Why wasn't that enough for her?

Ben couldn't get enough of Kayla.

One glimpse of her clothes plastered against her curves and his temperature soared. His blood boiled to the point that he needed to be doused with a Super Soaker himself.

The pile of work he needed to do would keep his mind focused and off Kayla.

Yeah, right. He hadn't stopped thinking about her since kissing her. Who was he kidding? She'd been on his mind since stepping aboard his ship.

He didn't get it. He tried to understand why. Tried and failed. She was one of the crew, a member of the expedition team and off limits. Not hard to understand.

But putting it into practice was another story.

He might treat her like one of the guys, but she wasn't. Never would be.

Ben had given up finding the perfect woman. Not only for him, but Madison, too. The perfect woman didn't exist. Kayla Waterton wasn't perfect, but she came damn close.

And that made it harder to ignore his attraction.

He concentrated on the e-mail from the Museum of Maritime History, a press release about the expedition's progress he'd downloaded. Nothing earth-shattering. Nothing that would make other salvage operations think they were any closer to finding the elusive *Izzy*.

Ben's eyes focused on Kayla's name, and his heart filled with pride. She should publish her research. It would make an even better book if she documented the entire expedition. That would give her a reason to stay on board during the recovery phase.

Kayla Waterton, noted maritime historian and founder of the Museum of Maritime History in Portland, Oregon.

Ben did a double take. He reread the line. He hadn't misread it.

Kayla didn't work for the museum; she *was* the museum.

Why hadn't she been up front and told him? Why hadn't she said anything for two weeks?

He wanted answers and he wanted them now.

With a printout of the press release in his hand, Ben headed to the control room. His footsteps thundered down the passageway. His pulse pounded in his throat. His temper rose with each step.

And that made him angrier. Kayla shouldn't have this ability to make him so upset. He wanted to be indifferent, not care about what she said or did. But he wasn't, and he cared too much. No longer.

He stormed into the control room. "I need to talk to Kayla."

She sat in front of the bank of monitors. "I'll be off in an hour and a half."

"Now."

Zach mouthed the word "go" and Kayla rose. She followed Ben out of the control room and into the hallway.

"What's going on?" she asked. "Is Madison—"

"She's fine. Asleep." He shoved the printout into Kayla's hands. "Here."

"It's a press release from the museum."

"Read it."

She read the e-mail. Her face paled. "You know."

He clenched his jaw. "Took me two weeks to figure

out the truth. Bet you've been laughing your tail off over that.''

''It's not like that.'' Worry creased her forehead. Kayla reached for him, but he jerked away. ''Please, let me explain.''

Too late. She'd kept the truth from him. Nothing more needed to be said. Ben folded his arms over his chest. ''Can I get some popcorn? This should be entertaining.''

She frowned, and for once he didn't care. ''When I arrived, I assumed you already knew who I was. But when you didn't and we weren't getting along, I thought it would be better if I withheld my true position at the museum. I didn't want to cause any problems.''

''You've been one big problem ever since you stepped on board. Why would this make a difference?''

Hurt flashed in her eyes.

Kayla took a deep breath. And another. ''I didn't want there to be a power struggle.''

''A power struggle?''

''Between you and me.'' Her eyes pleaded with him. ''How do you think it would have been if I came on board, tossed around my title and demanded you change coordinates?''

Ben didn't say anything, but he could imagine the scenario. It wouldn't have been pretty. Hell, it would have been a war.

''We were already butting heads and accomplishing nothing. I did what I thought best for the expedition.''

''How noble of you.''

''It was noble.'' She tilted her chin. ''I knew you were wasting valuable time and money. You know it now, too.''

She had a point. Maybe more than one. But she still hadn't told him the truth after he'd moved the search.

She'd had plenty of chances. Like after they'd kissed. "You could have told me once we started getting along."

She nodded. "I didn't think it was important."

"It is important." He lowered his voice. "I don't like secrets to begin with, but I hate any that affect me and my crew."

"I'm part of your crew. That's why I didn't want to say anything. Everyone treats me like I belong here." Her gaze filled with concern. "I've never had that before. And I like it. I really like it." She scratched her calf. "I didn't want that to change. I don't want it to change now."

"You were selfish."

Kayla nodded. "I've been selfish from the beginning."

Her admission surprised him. He'd expected her to deny it.

Her gaze met his. "Do you forgive me?"

He didn't like what she'd done, but he understood her logic. Things would have worked out differently had she been honest. Perhaps better, but the past was the past. They couldn't go back and change it. "I forgive you."

She rubbed the top of her left foot against the back of her calf. "Thank you."

"You're welcome." He felt a strange relief that he'd forgiven her. Now to forget. He'd always had a hard time with that. Just ask his ex-wife and his father. But Ben didn't like being disappointed by the people he cared about.

"Anything else I should know about?"

"Maybe."

His muscles tensed. "What do you mean, maybe?"

She pulled her necklace from beneath her sweatshirt.

"The necklace your father gave you?"

She nodded. "I didn't show you all my research."

"That doesn't surprise me."

"It has nothing to do with the location of the *Isabella,* so I didn't show you." Her eyes held no malice, no deceit. Only compassion, understanding and hope. "It has to do with one of the reasons I've been so selfish about this expedition."

"I'm listening." She was leading them to the *Izzy.* He owed her that much.

"In one of my father's journals, I found notes about the *Isabella* with symbols like these." She held up the talisman. "The writings matched. A few of the markings were identical."

"You think there's a connection?"

She nodded. "None of his other research had the markings, so it was particular to the *Isabella.*"

"You've got to know the odds of finding anything after so many years. The *Izzy's* been on the bottom for—"

"Centuries. I know." She sighed. "It must sound ridiculous, but it's my only clue. I have to follow through."

The hope he'd seen in her eyes echoed in her voice. Part of him wanted to make her see the futility of her search. But another part wanted to take her in his arms and help her find the answers she needed. "It's that important to you?"

She nodded. "I loved having my father all to myself, but I felt like a part of me, us, was missing. I used to fill the missing part up with my father's stories about mermaids, fairies and leprechauns. But those things never came to visit or have dinner with us. They didn't give hugs or kisses."

"They weren't real."

Her soft smile tugged at his heart. "They seemed real to me, but they weren't family."

"You don't have any other family?"

"I don't know." She sighed. "I don't even know where I was born or where my mother is buried. I have lots of questions and no answers."

She sounded like a lonely little girl who wanted to believe in Santa Claus and the Easter Bunny. He wanted not to care, but his heart ached for her. She was going to be disappointed. "The *Izzy* won't answer your questions."

"Probably not, but I may get another clue. Something to tell me where to look next." She glanced up at him. "Whether I find answers or not, the *Isabella* will bring me closer to my father. Finding the ship was his dream. Now it's mine."

Danger, danger. The red alarm light flashed in his mind. The siren blared in his head.

"What's your dream, Ben?"

"I don't have one. Not like you do."

"Finding the *Isabella* is a dream."

"It's a job." He gritted his teeth. "I'm not chasing a dream, I'm finding a ship."

"A treasure ship." She grinned. "Like your dad?"

"No. *Not* like my dad. I'm nothing like him." Ben sounded childish. He was acting that way, too. "My father dreams about a lot of things, but his dreams are nothing but a waste of time."

"Dreams are never a waste. They make each day worth living."

She was wrong. Ben's stomach knotted. "My ex-wife dreamed of being a movie star. When Madison was six months old, Lyssa got a part on a soap opera. It led to other roles, one in prime time. I offered to sell the operation to Wolf and be with her, but there wasn't enough room for both her dream and us.''

Kayla squeezed his shoulder. "That's horrible."

He shrugged, but the last thing he felt was indifference. "She was following her dream. That was more important than her daughter or her marriage."

"Your ex obviously didn't realize what a great thing she had." Kayla touched his cheek. The caress of her soft hand on his face nearly undid him. Ben drew strength from her gentle touch. He should back away, but he didn't want to. "Dreams are supposed to be shared. Otherwise they don't mean as much."

"Dreams are selfish." Both his father and ex-wife put their dreams first. Above family, above everything. Ben wondered why his mom still stuck by his dad after all this time. He thought about Madison and the price she would pay for her mother's dream. "They're no good."

"What a person does with a dream can make them seem bad, especially when it hurts others or leads to selfish choices." Compassion filled Kayla's voice. "But it's not always black or white."

"Yes, it is." He didn't dare dream. He wasn't going to be a failure like his father or a bad parent like his ex-wife. "Dreams lead to disappointment. That's why I need to make sure Madison grows up to be practical and responsible. It's like alcoholism running in a family. She's got the dream gene on both sides so I have to be extra careful. Dreams carry too high a price."

"The cost is worth it." Silver sparks danced in the depths of Kayla's gray-green eyes. "I've always been a dreamer. When I was growing up, kids teased me. I was different because I wanted to believe that anything was possible. I never fit in, I'll be the first to admit that, but no one tried to get to know the girl they called Kooky Kayla and Wacky Waterton. My classmates never looked beyond those labels. They never saw me. Kayla. And that's what hurt, but it wasn't enough to make me give up my dreams. I couldn't live without them.''

"What if your dreams don't come true?"

"Not all dreams are meant to." Her lips eased into a gentle smile. "The dream itself is what matters. Not whether it comes true or not."

Ben didn't buy that. Not for a second.

She leaned toward him. Her warm breath teased his neck. "It's never too late to dream."

Forget about dreams. Ben wanted to kiss her. More than he'd wanted anything in a long time. Too bad kissing was not only against the rules but also out of the question. Not even when he fell asleep tonight and dreamed.

Kayla had to be dreaming. What else could explain how wonderful this afternoon had been? Ben had forgiven her and they'd talked about dreams, about life, about a lot of things. But they hadn't kissed again. They'd come close, but it was better this way. He was going to help her find answers. She was going to help him dream. A fair trade.

Ben needed to regain his sense of wonder. Not only for himself, but for Madison, too.

Kayla was falling for him. It was getting harder to deny the obvious, even though nothing would come of it. Ben Mendoza was tall, dark and handsome, a sexy pirate who sent her pulse racing, but she'd come to realize he was so much more than a pretty face.

The more Kayla learned about him, the more she liked him. He was far from perfect. A little too stubborn, a little too wary, a lot too practical for his own good and hers. But those characteristics made him all the more real. She saw beneath his rough exterior to the caring man underneath. Patient, giving, loving. He was all those things and more.

She scratched her leg. If only Kayla could explain why she felt so strange as easily as she could rationalize her feelings for Ben. Her hips ached again. Her legs and feet, too. Her muscles felt tight and her skin itched. She'd broken out in a rash. Scaly patches on her legs. She'd taken an antihistamine in case it was an allergy.

But what would she be allergic to? Ben? She wasn't that lucky. Sunscreen? No, she'd used that brand before. Soap? No, she'd brought her own from home. Something in the ocean water? Maybe seaweed? No, that didn't make sense.

Kayla couldn't explain an allergy, but she'd thought of another explanation.

Lovesick.

Not that she was in love with Ben. Love wasn't an option in her life right now. She had too many questions to answer first. But she could live with an extreme case of "like."

Likesick. Didn't sound as good.

Maybe she was coming down with the flu. She felt a little hot and could have a temperature with the way she alternated between chills and hot flashes. But she couldn't afford to get sick.

Kayla padded her way to the sink, downed an ibuprofen and drank two glasses of water. She'd been thirsty all day. Too much sun? Probably too much Ben.

Funny how everything always came back to him.

Kayla smiled and took a step away from the sink. Her legs gave way. She hit the floor with a thud. Great. One thought of Ben and she'd turned into a swooning maiden. Macaroni legs. Or was that Jell-O? Probably the antihistamine. Those usually made her a little woozy.

She tried to stand, but her legs wouldn't support her weight. She crawled to her bed, pulled herself up and struggled to catch her breath.

What was happening?

Sweat beaded on her brow, dripped down her back. Hot. She was so hot.

Water. She needed water. Lots of water.

A knock sounded at the door.

Her throat burned. "It's open."

Ben stepped in. One look at her and his forehead wrinkled with concern. He raced to her side. "Kayla?"

"Water, please."

She downed the glass and asked for another. The burning ceased. She felt human again. "Thanks."

He touched her forehead with the back of his hand. "You're hot."

"I'm fine."

Ben raised a brow.

"I feel better now. It sort of comes and goes."

He sat next to her. With his weight on the mattress, she rolled toward him. Her thigh touched his. If she wasn't running a fever before, she was now. Her diagnosis of lovesick was true.

She scooted away. *Away* was a relative term. Calling her bed a twin was generous. At least she wasn't thigh-to-thigh with him now. Another two inches... "I got a little dehydrated. Nothing serious."

Forget about her legs and hips causing her pain. They weren't anything to be concerned about. Not when her heart and pulse and stomach were going crazy with Ben so close. She scratched her calf.

"You've been scratching your legs a lot."

"They itch," she said. "I thought it could be an allergy. I have a rash."

"Let me see."

His touch was as innocent as possible, but heat emanated from the spot of his hand and spread. When he removed his palm, she felt a chill. Boy, did she have it bad.

"There's no rash."

"What do you mean there's no—" She looked at her legs. The scaly patches had disappeared. "That's strange. They were just there."

"Do you want me to call a doctor?"

She smiled at the concern in his voice. "I doubt a doctor would make a house call out here."

"We have the satellite phone."

"I don't need a doctor. Get some liquids in me and I'll be good as new. Better than new."

"Promise?"

Her gaze met his. "I promise."

"I'll take your shift tonight."

"That isn't necessary."

"You don't have a choice." He used his I'm-in-charge-don't-talk-back tone. "If you're coming down with something, you need to rest. I don't want my entire crew to get sick."

"Or Madison," Kayla added.

"Or Madison."

"What about you?"

"I'll take my chances." His fingertips gently combed through her hair. She wondered if he did that when the other members of the crew got sick. "Do you need anything?" he asked.

"Besides the *Isabella?*"

One corner of his mouth lifted into a slight smile. He rose. "Let me tuck you in."

"Do you tuck in Wolf or Monk or Zach or Fitz or—"

"No."

"Then why—"

"You're cuter and smell a whole lot better."

His voice sent a ripple of awareness through her. "I don't want to be treated any differently than other crew members. The rules—"

"Are being broken tonight." He covered her with a sheet and kissed her forehead. "Sweet dreams."

Her eyelids felt heavy, but she wasn't ready to say good-night. If the rules weren't being enforced tonight... "Is that all?"

"I could tell you a story." She heard laughter in his voice. "That's what I do with Madison."

"I'm not Madison." Kayla mustered her courage. "Tonight you haven't been treating me like a member of your crew and I...I like it."

Ben sat. He reached for her and his calloused fingertip caressed her cheek, his touch as light as a whisper. Soothing and comforting. "So beautiful."

He pulled her onto his lap. The heartrending tenderness of his gaze made her bury her face against him. She shouldn't want this, want him.

"Kayla."

She glanced up. Desire filled his eyes. Desire for her. Knowing she'd put that look in his eyes made Kayla feel sexy, wanted. She felt so connected. Not so alone. Not so lost.

Before she could say a word, Ben lowered his mouth to her trembling lips. His initial touch was feather soft, but then he increased the pressure. She closed her eyes. More, she wanted more of him. All of him.

Don't do this, a little voice in her head warned, but Kayla didn't pull away. She didn't want to. Ben's arms circled her and she went willingly. Into his warmth and into his strength. He was so strong, so solid, so male. Kayla inhaled his soap-and-water scent and imprinted it on her memory. She wanted to remember everything about this moment.

Kayla curled her fingers in his hair. She kissed him back, her eagerness unfamiliar to herself. She didn't care. All that mattered was Ben and his kiss. Make that kisses. Hunger and need took control.

With Ben's kiss she found the answers to her questions, the realization of her dreams. She was swimming through a haze of feelings and desires. She wasn't ready to come out of the water just yet.

Ben drew the kiss to an end. Much too soon, but she wasn't about to complain. His dark eyes reflected a glimmer of light, a glint of wonder. Soon he would believe in dreams. "Was that better?"

She nodded. "Much."

"Sweet dreams."

Kayla snuggled against her pillow and smiled. "Thanks to you."

Chapter Nine

"Come on, Kayla." Madison tugged on her arm. "Uncle Wolf filled up the pool for us again."

The short climb to the bow hurt Kayla's thighs, but she felt better this morning. A good night's sleep had worked wonders. A good-night kiss had her wondering.

"I like your swimsuit," Madison said.

"Thank you." Kayla had tossed the lime-green bikini into her suitcase as an afterthought, but was so relieved she had it with her now. Her one-piece had felt uncomfortable when she put it on so she'd opted for the bikini with ties on the side. No elastic to bother her aching hips. "I like yours, too."

"It's pink." Madison was an adorable picture of pink from head to toe with coordinating hat, towel, life jacket, swimsuit and towel. Cotton candy never looked so pink. Bubble gum, either. Even Baby Fifi was wrapped in her own pink towel. "Pink is my favorite color."

"Really?"

"Yes, it's— Daddy!" Madison threw herself into Ben's arms.

Kayla wished she could do the same. She hadn't seen him since he'd tucked her in last night, but she still tasted the sweet flavor of his kiss.

Madison placed her hands on her hips. "Why aren't you working, Daddy?"

"Because I had to see to my favorite girl." He waved a pink bottle in the air. "Did you put on sunscreen?"

Madison pursed her lips. "I forgot."

He ruffled her hat. "Good thing I didn't."

"That's because you're the daddy."

Ben's soft smile tugged at Kayla's heart.

He rubbed sunscreen on Madison. "All done, princess."

"Thank you." She kissed his cheek. "Your turn, Kayla."

The thought of Ben rubbing lotion on her made Kayla tingle all over. "I'll pass."

"Daddy's really good at this."

"I'm sure he is." Kayla swallowed around the Atlantic-size lump in her throat. "I, uh, I'm fine."

Madison pursed her lips. "You can't go in the water without sunscreen. That's the rule, isn't it, Daddy?"

"Those are the rules." Mischief gleamed in his eyes. "Come here."

Jumping overboard was a safer option. "It's okay. I don't burn."

"Rules are rules." The laughter in his voice matched that in his eyes.

Real funny. Last night he'd broken the rules. So had she. Kayla could only imagine the price she'd pay if anyone found out. "I can do it myself."

"What if you miss a spot?" He feigned concern. "I'd never be able to live with myself."

"I never knew you were so altruistic."

"There are lots of things you don't know about me."

Kayla was sure of it. She already felt itchy and shivery. Being near Ben made it worse. Maybe she *was* allergic to him after all. Self-preservation was a strong instinct.

"Can I get in the water, Daddy?" Madison asked.

"Jump right in." Ben rubbed lotion between his palms, and Kayla's muscles tensed. "Relax, this isn't going to hurt."

That's what she was afraid of. She was getting in too deep. Time to head for the shallow end before she got in over her head. "You don't have to—"

"Can't mess with the rules." He touched her shoulders and she stiffened. "What would Madison say?"

A glance showed the little girl splashing in the pool. "She's too busy playing to notice."

"But I'll know." He smoothed the lotion over Kayla's back. "And after last night…"

After last night she wasn't sure what to think. Her heart said one thing, her head another. "We broke the rules last night."

His rule-breaking kiss would be a part of her memory for a long time. Possibly forever.

He kneaded her upper arms. "That's why I have to set a good example now."

A good example was one thing, but this was…great. Wonderful. Amazing. His hands were large and strong and calloused. Rough almost, though his touch was anything but. Muscles relaxed. Stress evaporated. Tension… Two out of three wasn't bad.

The smart thing would be to say thank-you and get in

the pool with Madison. But Kayla never did the smart thing where Ben was concerned, and at the moment she didn't care.

Kayla closed her eyes and enjoyed the sensations his touch brought. His hot breath caressed her neck, sending a pleasurable shiver down her spine.

He massaged the lotion into her back with experienced hands. He knew what he was doing, and she would never look at putting sunscreen on as a chore again. Heat pooled low in her abdomen and emanated out.

"Feel good?" he whispered.

Much too good. She couldn't speak, didn't want to try. She nodded instead.

Madison giggled and splashed water at them. "Hurry up. You're missing all the fun."

"She doesn't understand about adult fun," Ben whispered. "I'm having fun. Are you?"

He was flirting with her. She liked it, but that didn't make it right. Kayla swallowed. Hard.

"Are you coming, Kayla?" Madison asked.

Kayla didn't answer. She couldn't. She didn't want to move. She wanted to stay like this forever.

"Are you coming?" Ben's suggestive tone teased, aroused.

She was drifting into even deeper waters. She hoped someone threw her a life preserver. The sooner the better. "Be right there, Madison," Kayla finally called out.

"I'm not finished," Ben said.

Kayla's heart leapt with anticipation. She was being silly. This was about sunscreen, nothing else. Yet her pulse quickened. She felt light-headed and couldn't blame the medicine she'd taken last night. Enough was enough. Time to put an end to this. The rules may have been broken, but they hadn't changed. "I am."

"Your legs—"

"Are fine."

"More than fine, but I won't argue the point."

She grabbed the sunscreen from his hand and lathered her legs with the white lotion. It stung, but she managed not to grimace. "Satisfied?"

A smug smile formed on his lips. "Got your bikini bottoms in a twist, I see."

"Now you can go away."

"Yes, Daddy," Madison said. "Go away. We want to play."

Kayla blushed when she realized Madison could see and hear them. "I'm sorry, I forgot—"

"No big deal." He took the sunscreen from Kayla, leaned toward her and grinned. "But once you're finished having fun with my daughter, make it up to me by having some fun with me."

It was all she could do to keep her mouth from gaping open. Didn't he remember the rules?

Had he forgotten all the rules?

Either that or Ben was losing his mind. He studied the search grid. Halfway through the search area and no significant targets yet. He didn't care. And that was bad.

He should care. Care a lot. But his mind was focused on one thing—Kayla Waterton.

He'd been wrong. She was no angel. She'd pretended to have wings and a halo, but she was really a siren in disguise. How else could he explain his behavior? Breaking rules without a thought to the consequences? He was acting like a teenager in hormonal hyperdrive.

Not even his crew had had it this bad. Well, maybe Monk.

Pathetic, that's what Ben had become. A pathetic, panting puppy. And Kayla was holding his leash.

Attraction, he could live with. Lust, he knew how to handle. Chemistry, he understood. But this went deeper. To a place he didn't want it to go, a place inside him off limits to everyone except Madison and possibly his mother.

"Boss," Gray said over the intercom. "Get down here."

"On my way."

Ben jogged to the control room, his mind still on Kayla. Even if he were interested in pursuing her, it wouldn't work. She lived in Portland. She had a home and her work. Not to mention a damn museum. She also had dreams. Her dreams included the *Isabella,* but not him or Madison. Kayla wanted to find answers, not a family. He wasn't going to go through that again.

He entered the control room. "What's up?"

Vance smiled. "Check this out, boss."

Ben studied the images on the monitors. "Measurements?"

"It's the right length," Gray said.

"See the debris field surrounding the center mass?" Vance added.

The familiar rush of adrenaline surged through Ben. He leaned forward. "It could be anything."

Vance rose. "It's three hundred meters from where Kayla thought it would be."

Hot damn. "You get all the—"

"Got everything," Wolf answered. "Want me to get her?"

The target had all the correct characteristics, but Ben

didn't want Kayla to be disappointed again. "Let's wait until we know more. Don't want to get her hopes up if it's not—"

"You like her, don't you, boss?" Gray asked.

Wolf flashed him a silent warning.

"Just asking a question," Gray said. "I might not be the sharpest hook in the tackle box when it comes to females, but I'm not blind. I see the way she looks at the boss."

"Me, too," Vance added.

"It's…nothing." And that's how it would remain. Ben glanced around. "You boys—"

"Don't mind." Wolf nodded. "You weren't part of the bet. We heard what Kayla said. She's had her eye on you from the beginning, boss."

"You think so?" Ben asked.

All three men agreed, but he trusted Wolf the most.

"Go for it, boss." Gray grinned. "The Little Bit needs a mommy."

Ben slid into a chair and leaned back. This was going to take some thought, but no matter what he decided, new rules were going to be needed.

Ben had wreaked havoc on Kayla's senses, on her muscular and nervous systems, too. Thank goodness the water in the kiddie pool was as effective as a cold shower.

Not to mention how nice it felt on her legs.

Her hips and legs still hurt, but sitting in the saltwater was refreshing and relieved some of the pain. So did Madison. She was a bundle of energy and grins. They volleyed a beach ball back and forth. Kayla reached for the ball, but a knife-edged pain sliced through her side and she missed. The ball flew across the deck.

Madison giggled. "I'll get it."

"Be careful."

As Madison picked up the ball, Kayla felt a tightness in her legs. Her bikini bottoms cut into her hips, and she loosened the strings holding them together. A weird pulling sensation took over. She touched her legs, but that made it worse.

"Ow." She tried to grip the bottom of the pool. It felt as if the skin was being pulled off her leg. She gritted her teeth. Her eyes watered.

"Kayla?" Madison's voice sounded shaky and scared.

"I'm…I'll be fine, sweetie." Kayla struggled for a breath. It was as if someone the size of Wolf was standing on her chest. "Just a…cramp. An—*oow.*"

"Want a drink?"

"Please. Water."

Pain seared through her. So hot. Burning.

Air, she needed air.

The slight breeze brought a moment of relief. It wasn't enough. She gasped for a breath.

What was happening?

She rested her head on the edge of the pool and fought the rising panic. She had to keep her eyes open and watch Madison. It was so hard. Everything hurt. Tears rolled down her cheeks.

Madison handed her a bottle of water. "Here."

Kayla opened the bottle and gulped. The cool water soothed her throat. Calmed her nerves. Eased the pain.

"Can I have a tail, too?" Madison asked.

Kayla took another swig from the bottle.

Two little lines formed above Madison's nose. "Yours is pretty, but I'd like mine to be pink."

Kayla felt almost normal. "What would you like to be pink, sweetie?"

"My mermaid tail."

Madison was so adorable. Kayla smiled. "Pink it is, then."

"Can I touch your tail?"

What a vivid imagination. "Go ahead."

As Madison climbed into the pool, Kayla drank the rest of her water. She felt the little girl's touch. It didn't hurt. Kayla glanced down and spewed the water out of her mouth.

Madison giggled. "Do that again."

All Kayla could do was stare. She sat frozen, unable to think or move. Her mind reeled. Her emotions spun out of control. Her world shifted on its axis.

This can't be happening. She wasn't seeing this. Panic took hold of her. It can't be—

"Your tail is blue and green and silvery. How come it's not pink?"

Her heart twisted with fear. Kayla trembled. "I—I…"

Madison rubbed it. "It feels funny."

Kayla didn't want to touch it; she didn't want to look at it. She didn't want to frighten Madison, but Kayla couldn't stop shaking. She gasped for air.

Where were her feet? Her legs? Her bikini bottoms? She blinked. The tail shimmered in the sunlight. She had a tail. A tail! A mermaid tail. With scales and everything.

It wasn't real. It couldn't be real.

Madison glanced up. "Wait until my daddy finds out."

No one could know. Especially Ben. A wave of apprehension washed over Kayla. She swallowed around the lump in her throat and found her voice. "Let's not tell anyone about this."

Madison's eyes grew as wide as doubloons. "You mean, keep it a secret?"

"Yes, a secret," Kayla whispered. Her pulse beat erratically. She thought her chest might explode from the thundering of her heart. "Between you and me."

"Do we cross our hearts?"

"Let's cross our hearts." Kayla struggled to carry on a coherent conversation. It wasn't a joke. It wasn't a dream. Her legs were gone and she had a tail. The knowledge twisted and turned inside her.

"What about the dolphins?"

Her brain had short-circuited. She couldn't think straight. "Dolphins?"

Madison pointed to the water. A group of dolphins swam next to the boat. "They need to cross their hearts, too."

Kayla bit back the laughter threatening to overwhelm her. She had to remain in control. Hysteria would accomplish nothing. "I don't think they heard us."

She crawled out of the pool. Not an easy task without any legs and a tail she couldn't control. She flopped onto the deck. It gave new meaning to the phrase "a fish out of water."

Madison hopped out of the pool. She placed Kayla's bikini bottoms on a deck chair. "Are you okay?"

Kayla didn't know how to answer. Saying she was fine seemed like an overstatement, but at least she'd pulled herself together. Well, sort of. "Could you bring me my towel, please?"

Madison ran, picked up her towel and handed it to her.

"Thanks." Kayla dried the tail. A tail. Her tail.

"You're a mermaid like in 'lantis."

"Like Atlantis," Kayla echoed.

She touched the silver talisman around her neck. This had to be the secret. The one her father was going to tell her when she turned sixteen. Was this why he wanted her to stay out of the ocean?

It was starting to make some sense.

Okay, maybe not sense, but the pieces were coming together. This had to be her father's big secret. She couldn't imagine learning a bigger secret than finding out you were a fish.

Wait a minute. She wasn't a fish. She couldn't be a mermaid. She was Kayla Waterton, a maritime historian.

She sat in the sun for what seemed like forever but was really only half an hour. She couldn't believe no one had come by. Shift change? Or an extreme case of luck. Magically, her tail disappeared and her legs returned. Thank goodness she and Madison were out here alone. Kayla wrapped the towel around her like a skirt.

"How did you do that?" Madison asked.

"I'm not sure."

She touched Kayla's legs. It still didn't hurt. "You're not a mermaid anymore."

"I'm not a mermaid." Saying the words was as much for her benefit as Madison's. Kayla wasn't a mermaid. She touched the talisman again. She'd never felt more alone in her life.

Madison hugged her. "It'll be okay."

Kayla held on to the little girl in her arms, soaking up her warmth and her strength. "Thank you."

"Did you have fun playing in the pool?" Ben asked.

Kayla let go of Madison and clutched the towel around her waist. She didn't want it to slip off. She looked around nervously and saw that her bikini bottoms had slipped off the deck chair where Ben couldn't see them.

"Daddy, Daddy." Madison jumped up and down. "Kayla's a…"

Her heart pounded in her throat. She couldn't blame a three-year-old for not keeping a secret.

"A what, princess?" Ben asked.

Madison stared at Kayla and smiled. "She's a girl."

"Really?" He ruffled Madison's wet hair. "Thanks for letting me know."

Relief washed over Kayla. Her secret was safe. For now. But it made her wonder. What would Ben say when he learned she wasn't only a girl, she was also a fish?

"Don't you like fish?" Ben sat across from Kayla in the dining room and stared at her full plate. She hadn't eaten a bite of her dinner. Something was wrong. She always ate whatever Stevie made and usually went back for seconds. "It's fresh. Fitz and Zach caught them today."

Her face paled. "I'm not hungry."

"Do you feel okay?"

She nodded. "Any other questions?"

Madison shifted in her chair. "Can I have more bread?"

Ben raised a brow. "Is that the correct way to ask for something?"

"May I have more bread, please?" Madison asked.

"Yes, you may," Ben said.

"I'll get it." Kayla buttered another roll for Madison and placed it on her plate. "Here you go, sweetie."

"Thank you." Madison grinned. "It's the way I like it."

Kayla tapped the end of Madison's button nose. "I'm so glad."

Madison giggled. Kayla joined in.

Watching the two of them laugh together did funny things to his heart. Madison flourished under Kayla's attention. And Kayla...she would make a good mom.

His two girls. His.

Soothing warmth filled him. It was as if the three of them were already a real family. It could work. But the hows and the whens boggled his mind.

Madison counted her peas.

"How was learning time?" Ben asked.

She grinned. "Uncle Wolf helped me make a world. We painted it blue and cut out coun...continents."

"I can't wait to see it." Another work of art to add to his wall. Ben smiled. "Did you work on letters and numbers?"

"We counted and I sent an e-mail to Grandma and Grandpa." Her eyes lit up. "Kayla helped me."

He glanced at Kayla. "You helped her?"

"Eugene was busy debugging his program." She touched the top of Madison's hand. "We had fun and learned lots, didn't we?"

Madison nodded, her eyes twinkling. "Lots, Daddy. Did you have a good day?"

Ben wiped his mouth with a napkin. "Yes. We found a couple of targets."

Kayla held her fork midair. "Anything significant?"

He shrugged. "Could be, but we want to finish mowing before we investigate."

Kayla studied the food on her plate. "Good, I mean, that's great."

Her voice sounded enthusiastic, but he thought she'd be more excited. She seemed distracted. Maybe she had the same concern as he did. If it turned out to be the *Izzy,* how much longer would Kayla stay?

Kayla had been patient during her afternoon shift and all through dinner. Now it was time. She had the privacy she needed to discover some answers.

She was a historian, not a scientist, but the best way to understand what was happening to her was to experiment. She'd borrowed a stopwatch from Wolf. She had her journal and a mechanical pencil to record observations. Curiosity had replaced the terror of the unknown. She needed to know how this all worked.

Up on the "beach," she sat in the kiddie pool of saltwater and clicked the stopwatch. The seconds ticked by. The transformation occurred faster this time. Some pulling, a little tightness and a bit of compression. Not as much pain as the first time. No struggle for air. She jotted the changes.

A membrane formed between her legs. Another joined her feet. Scales appeared, overlapping one another and taking the place of her skin from her belly button down. And she had tiny, barely noticeable gills. She hit the stopwatch and recorded the time.

Flipping her tail, Kayla took a deep breath. She was a mermaid. She felt a little detached from the realization. She wasn't sure how to act. How did one react when they learned they weren't human? Her entire life people had said she was different. If they only knew...

She crawled out of the pool, dried off with a towel and hit the stopwatch again. Moonlight shimmered off the scales, iridescent silver with flashes of green and blue. Her tail was pretty—stunning, actually. Even if it wasn't pink. Kayla smiled and touched her necklace.

Madison's comment this morning made Kayla realize

how her father had prepared her for this. His stories about Atlantis had been real, a way to pave the way for the truth.

Kayla remembered how he spoke of children being enveloped in the sea—the process of becoming a mer when a child turned three. They had waited until that age because of the pain involved with the first transformation. That's what he had called it. They didn't want the child to become frightened of the water. Madison was three and that seemed too young. Dad must have thought so, too, Kayla realized. That must be why he waited. Or maybe the reason was due to her mother's death when she was two. But if her mother was a mermaid, too, how could she have drowned?

Kayla checked her tail. It was still there after fifteen minutes.

She recalled another story about a battle waged between two factions within Atlantis—the swimmers and the breathers. The swimmers believed humans were dangerous and feared the world's discovery. The breathers feared isolation would destroy Atlantis. A battle had ensued. Which had her family been? Breathers since they'd left Atlantis?

Too many questions. She needed to concentrate on those she could answer.

She heard a noise coming from the water. Kayla glanced through the railing and saw a dolphin chattering. "If you're talking to me, I don't speak dolphin."

That didn't stop the dolphin. The chatter continued.

She smiled. "If you see any other mermaids out there, could you please send them this way? I really need someone to explain a few things."

The dolphin swam away.

The membrane of Kayla's tail parted, the gills subsided and her legs appeared. She hit the stopwatch. Thirty minutes—the total time it took for her tail to vanish. She noted the steps in her journal and prepared for the next experiment. She climbed back in the pool. The tail appeared quicker this time with almost no pain.

Time for the big one. Kayla wanted to see if the gills worked. All she had to do was put her head underwater and breathe. She tried to go under. The water covered her face and she sat up. She'd been through enough today. Might as well save something for tomorrow.

Kayla crawled out of the pool. One last experiment remained tonight. How long would it take for her tail to disappear without drying off with a towel first?

"Come here, princess." Ben picked up his bundle of sunshine and smiles, the light of his life, most especially his heart, and carried her to her bed. "You know what time it is."

Madison crawled under her princess-patterned bedding with Baby Fifi in her arms. "Where's Kayla?"

"She's working."

"Is she going to live with us?"

Talk about a loaded question. "Kayla lives in Oregon."

"Our place is good."

"Yes, but—"

"She needs to be close to the ocean. She needs to stay with us."

Madison made it sound so simple. Maybe it was.

"I love Kayla." Madison pursed her lips and looked much older than three. "Do you love her, Daddy?"

Ben didn't know how to answer. His feelings for Kayla were as complicated as the ownership rights to treasure found in a shallow water wreck. She was beautiful, caring, giving. The list went on. But what did that mean tonight, tomorrow, the next day?

"I like Kayla." His chest tightened. "She's…nice."

An understatement if he'd ever heard one.

"So you want her to stay, too."

It wasn't a question. Madison sounded so much like him. Ben smiled. "It's not that simple, princess."

"I'm going to wish it." She tilted her chin. "If you wish hard enough, you can make it come true."

Now she sounded like Kayla. Ben laughed. "Did Kayla tell you that?"

Madison nodded. "Kayla told me about Atlantis and the mermaids who live there. Mermaids are real, Daddy."

He ruffled her hair. "Honey, those things may be fun to hear about, but they're make-believe. They aren't real."

"Kayla said if you believe in your heart, they can be real." Madison's eyes twinkled. "When I grow up, I want to be a mermaid with a pink tail. And I can marry a mermaid boy."

She's three. It shouldn't matter. But it did to Ben. "Right now, you need to go to bed." He tucked the blanket around her and kissed her good-night. "I love you."

"I love you, Daddy."

"Sweet dreams, princess."

She smiled. "I'm going to dream about mermaids."

Mermaids again? Madison had mentioned seeing one a while ago, but this mermaid infatuation of hers started after Kayla arrived. Ben didn't like it. Kayla had promised she would be careful around Madison.

He had to speak with her about Madison. He didn't want to do it, but he had no choice. If anything was going to work out between them, she was going to have to stop filling Madison's head with these crazy fantasies. New rules were needed, and Ben knew the first one— no mermaid tales allowed.

"Kayla."

The sound of Ben's voice startled her. She wanted to tell him what was happening to her. She needed his support; she needed him.

Show him your tail.

No, that would overwhelm him. He was so practical. Learning to dream again was going to be hard enough for Ben. This bordered on the impossible. She would have to ease in slowly, explain about mermaids and help him see the possibilities.

She scooted on the deck, pulled herself into a chair and covered the tail with towels. She looked normal except for the fin at the bottom of her tail. Kayla adjusted a towel. "Up here."

Ben's tall, dark figure emerged from the shadows. He moved with an easy grace. "What are you doing?"

"The water feels good on my legs."

"Do they still hurt?"

The concern in his voice touched her. "They're better." Different, considering she had no feet, but better in that they no longer hurt. A smile tugged at her lips.

"What?" he asked.

"It's nothing." She stared at him, at the inherent strength in his face. She wanted to rely on his strength, to have him help her through this. "I—I'm happy you're here."

He nodded. "I don't know what's happening between us, but I know, whatever it is, I don't want it to stop."

Her heart swelled with joy. "I feel the same way."

"Good." A muscle in his jaw twitched. "But there's something…"

A big something, but she didn't think he was talking about her tail. "What is it?"

"Madison."

"Do you think she'll have a problem if we—" Kayla struggled for the correct word "—date?"

"No. She loves you." His hair ruffled in the breeze. "But I'm worried about her. Remember how we talked about not telling her stories?"

"Yes, but having an active imagination is healthy for a child."

He pressed his lips together. "You said you would be careful."

She hesitated, torn by conflicting emotions. The strongest of which was guilt. "I've tried."

"It hasn't worked. Tonight she told me she wanted to be a mermaid. She seems to believe it can happen."

Kayla's heart thumped so loudly she was certain Ben could hear it. She chose her words carefully. "I wanted to be a mermaid when I was a little girl."

"But you're not a mermaid, you're a maritime historian."

The air whooshed from her lungs. Kayla was too shocked by what he'd said to do or say anything.

"I don't want Madison believing something so ridiculous is possible."

But it was possible. Mermaids were real. She knew it. So did Madison. A tumble of thoughts ran through her mind. She had to tell him the truth. "Ben—"

"You know how I feel." Hurt gleamed in his eyes. Pain from his past that needed to heal. "I won't have my daughter turned into a starry-eyed dreamer."

Kayla had to make him understand. "This isn't about dreams."

"What else would you call a mermaid?"

Me. Her throat clogged with emotion. She was scared. She didn't want to lose Ben or Madison. But that's what Kayla feared would happen if he learned the truth too soon.

"I won't have her walking around with her head in the clouds. Chasing unrealistic dreams. Unable to cope with daily life." He brushed his hand through his hair. "Both my father and Lyssa are like that. I don't want Madison to be the same."

Kayla had never felt so defeated in her life. Especially when she was unprepared to fight back. "Don't forget I'm a dreamer."

"You're different."

Yes, she was. But Ben wasn't ready to accept that. Not fully. Until he believed in dreams and possibilities, he would never understand. She could either accept that or not.

She sighed. "Are you worried about Madison being a dreamer or are you really worried one day she might chase one of those dreams and leave you?"

"I don't want her to be hurt."

Kayla wanted to believe him. "You can't protect her forever."

"I can protect her now." Ben's gaze sought hers, his eyes compelling and magnetic. She forced herself not to fall even deeper under his spell. "And I want your help. We can do it…together."

She felt so alone, and Ben wanted her. It was hard for her to believe after all she'd been through today. "Together?"

"I want you to stay and be a permanent member of

the crew." He laced his fingers with hers. "That will give us a chance to figure out the rest."

"The rest?"

"The three of us being a family. You, me and Madison." His gaze held hers. "With you, I'm beginning to believe anything is possible."

A family. It was beyond Kayla's wildest dreams. Ben had tossed her a life preserver—make that a lifeline. She wanted to hold on with both hands and never let go.

And she wouldn't.

Kayla would help Ben see dreams weren't something to fear. She would teach him to appreciate the goodness and joy dreams brought to one's life and be open to the possibilities.

Possibilities that included the existence of mermaids.

"Yes." She could barely breathe, but this time she didn't mind. "Yes, I'd like that very much."

Chapter Ten

"Hurry." Ben led Kayla to the control room. Holding her hand seemed so right, so normal. The way it was meant to be. Last night they'd talked until it was time for her shift. The more he learned about her, the better he felt. This was going to work. All of it.

"What's going on?" she asked.

"Be patient." He stopped outside the door. "I wanted to say something before... It's just... You've changed my life. And I know it's only going to get better." He kissed her on the lips. "Thank you."

Her forehead wrinkled. "I'm confused."

"Hold that thought." Ben pulled open the door. A rush of cold air greeted him, as did the smiling faces of the crew and Madison. Everyone was here. "The guest of honor has arrived."

"Hey, Kayla." Monk sat in the pilot's seat. He controlled the ROV, the remotely operated vehicle Ben and Wolf had designed and affectionately named GOTCHA. "I'm all set, boss."

Ben glanced at Vance. Nothing was going to happen without the marine archeologist's okay. "Vance?"

"The artifact's location has been fully documented." Vance grinned. "You're not going to want to see the bill for all the stills. We've been taking pictures all morning."

That was good enough for Ben. "Go get it, Monk."

"Would someone please tell me what's going on?" Kayla asked.

"In a minute, hon," Ben said.

Everyone in the room, including Kayla, stared at him. The curiosity was thick enough to stop an anchor. Ben ignored it.

He stared at the monitor. "Careful, Monk."

"Don't forget, boss, I'm known for my delicate touch." Monk manipulated GOTCHA toward the artifact. "Come on, darlin'. Come to Papa."

Ben watched the mechanical arm lift the bell. A cloud of silt rose from the ocean bottom and blurred the picture on the monitor. As the cloud settled, he saw the artifact in the basket. "Good job, Monk."

Kayla touched Madison's shoulder. "That looks like a—"

"It's a bell, Daddy."

Ben smiled. "Yes, it is."

Kayla's gaze met his. "Is it from the—"

"We'll know in an hour and a half when the GOTCHA surfaces." Ben still didn't want to get her hopes up. But he was going to make sure the champagne was chilled. Just in case.

It was the longest hour and a half of Kayla's life. If the ship turned out to be the *Isabella*, she would realize her father's dream. One of her dreams, too. She held on to her talisman. For luck.

"Why didn't you tell me?" she asked Ben as they waited on deck for GOTCHA's return.

"We still don't know what we've found." He caressed her cheek. "You haven't missed anything except documenting the site this morning, and you needed to sleep, anyway."

She smiled. "You were worried about me."

"A little."

From his tone, she realized it was more than a little. Her heart filled with love for him. He would come around about fairy tales, about dreams, about mermaids.

She was a mermaid.

With everything going on she'd forgotten. Or rather pushed it to the back of her mind.

He put his arm around her. "It's almost time."

Kayla nodded. She liked that Ben wasn't afraid to show affection in front of the rest of the crew. No one minded. No one held a grudge. Monk had told her he'd seen it coming. This was going to work. She knew it in her heart.

The crane lifted GOTCHA out of the water. The basket containing the bell hung underneath.

Her heart pounded. This could be it. This could be the bell from the *Isabella*.

The men worked to get the ROV on board. A combination of white gook and saltwater poured out and splashed on the deck. Kayla stayed out of the way. She was excited to see the bell, but she didn't want to get wet, so she stood back.

Fitz videotaped the happenings, and he wasn't using a camcorder. No, this looked professional. Kayla realized the crew also wore matching orange jumpsuits with an *Xmarks Explorer* logo. How things had changed in less than two hours.

Vance paced on the deck. He had a container, what looked like a glorified ice chest with wheels, ready for the bell. He'd been awake all night preparing the lab to receive and preserve artifacts in case they brought any to the surface.

The thought of artifacts from the *Isabella* on display at the museum sent a shiver of anticipation down her spine. This would be her way of fulfilling her father's dream. An *Isabella* exhibit in his name. *Please let this be it.*

The men crowded around the bell, pushing and shoving to get a good look.

"What does it say?"

"Get out of my way."

"Can you read it?"

"Hey, I can't see."

The guys acted more like a bunch of little boys who'd found something at a playground than a team of highly skilled salvage technicians. Kayla smiled and backed away. She was worried about the saltwater still pouring out and getting everything wet. She couldn't afford to change into a mermaid in front of everyone. She wasn't about to fulfill one dream and lose another.

"Back off, boys," Ben ordered. He pulled Kayla toward the bell. "You need to see this, too."

She hesitated, torn between wanting to see the bell and her fear of the water.

"Come on," he said.

Kayla watched where she stepped and moved forward. As she stared at the bell, a lump formed in her throat. She thought about her father, about the pirate Luis Serrano and his love, Ana Delgado. Emotion rendered her speechless.

Ben's eyes brimmed with tears. "You do the honors, Kayla."

She swallowed hard. "I-s-a-b-e-l-l-a." The name was engraved on the bell. "It's from the *Isabella*."

He hugged her. "You found her."

Behind Kayla a champagne cork popped. "We found her."

Ben smiled. "Yes, we did."

"Daddy. I'm done sleeping. Daddy?" Madison waited for her daddy to come. She looked at the clock. A two, a one and a five.

"Time to get up." She kissed Baby Fifi's forehead. "I like Kayla. She tells me stories and has a tail. I want a tail."

Madison slid out of bed, put on her pink life vest and connected the plastic buckles. She grabbed Baby Fifi off the bed. "I want to be a mermaid. Do you want to be a mermaid, Baby Fifi?" Madison headed out of her cabin.

On deck, she found her pool almost empty. Most of the water had spilled out. She needed water to get a tail. That's how Kayla had done it. Madison headed toward the stern. She tried to stick her feet over the edge and into the water, but she couldn't hold on to the rail and Baby Fifi.

"Once I get my tail, I'll help you get yours." Madison set her baby doll on the deck. "Don't cry. I'll be right back."

Water splashed her. Madison stuck her foot out a little farther and—

She fell overboard and landed with a splash. She coughed and spit out a mouthful of icky-tasting water. "Daddy!"

Sounded like trouble. The frantic chatter from a dolphin made every one of Kayla's nerve endings go on alert. Fresh out of the shower, Kayla put on her panties. She grabbed her bra, but dropped it to the floor.

There it was again.

More chatter. She felt almost connected to the dolphin, but that made no sense. Unless it had something to do with her being a mermaid. No, she was imagining a nonexistent bond.

The noise got louder.

The dolphin wasn't happy. It sounded...troubled. Concerned. Worried. Kayla wasn't sure how she knew that. If only she had a clue what the dolphin wanted, but the communication was emphatic, not telepathic.

Maybe the dolphin was hungry or lonely. Whatever the reason, Kayla's uneasiness increased. She had to get on deck. Now.

She left the bra on the floor, pulled on the orange jumpsuit the crew had given to her the day they found the *Isabella* and slipped on her shoes.

She hurried outside and bumped into Wolf. The burly man furrowed his brows. "Have you seen Madison?"

"Not since lunchtime." Kayla glanced at her watch. "Isn't it still her naptime?"

"I went to wake her up early to see a school of dolphins, but she wasn't in her cabin."

Worry flashed through Kayla. She was overreacting. Madison knew the rules. She was supposed to stay in bed until someone came to get her. "Ben must have gotten her."

"Maybe." Wolf didn't sound convinced, and the dolphin was sounding more agitated. "I'm going to find Ben."

"I'll look around."

"She might leave her cabin, but she wouldn't go on deck by herself."

Kayla nodded. The dolphin's chatter was getting worse, more insistent. She had trouble thinking straight. "Do you hear that?"

"What?"

"Nothing," she said.

But as Wolf headed inside, she knew the dolphin was trying to tell her something.

Why didn't a handbook come with the tail? Or a few classes in Mer 101? The stories her father told had left a large gap in her mer knowledge. And she didn't know who could teach her what she needed to know.

A dolphin jumped out of the water. Kayla's concern rose. He jumped again. No need to rationalize her feelings. Something was definitely wrong. She ran toward the dolphin. The sight of a doll near the rail made her skid to a stop.

Baby Fifi.

An all-consuming emptiness grabbed hold of her and refused to let go. Kayla couldn't move; she couldn't breathe. Her entire focus was on Madison and where she might be. A lump burned in her throat. She tried to swallow around it but couldn't. Tears stung her eyes and she blinked them back. She couldn't cry. She had to help. She had to do something.

"Madison!" Kayla called. And called again.

The dolphin slapped his nose against the water.

"I understand," Kayla said. "She's in the water."

She scanned the horizon but couldn't see anything. If

Madison wasn't wearing a life jacket…a sinking feeling in Kayla's stomach threatened to overwhelm her.

"Madison!"

Nothing.

Find her.

Kayla wasn't sure where the feeling came from. Herself or the dolphin. But it was strong, powerful. Yet she stood frozen. Afraid for Madison, afraid for herself. She was a mermaid, but she didn't know what that meant. How could she find Madison?

Uncertainty wreaked havoc in her mind.

But Madison needed her help.

So much was at stake. She'd finally found a place where she belonged. A family. A man to love. The truth would ruin it. The truth would change…everything.

Save her.

The feeling intensified. Overpowered Kayla. She stared at the dolphin. More chatter. She recognized something in the dolphin's dark eyes—compassion, understanding, concern. Kayla kicked off her shoes. They clattered to the deck.

She had to find Madison.

Kayla grabbed the railing.

How would she do this?

The sound of heavy footsteps and frantic calls for Madison from Ben and the rest of the crew filled the air. The jagged pain of their panicked voices was like a knife to Kayla's heart.

How could she not do this? She climbed over the railing.

"Kayla!" Ben ran toward her. "Stop!"

"I found Baby Fifi on deck," Kayla explained. "Madison's in the water, Ben. I don't know how I know…"

Silence.

It was as if time had stopped for that instant.

She saw the exact moment the news hit Ben. Blood drained from his face. He looked out at the ocean. The pain on his face told Kayla he didn't see anything but water. He grabbed the rail and started to hop over until Wolf pulled him back.

Ben fought the big man. "Let me go."

"No," Wolf said.

"She's out there." Ben's anguish brought tears to Kayla's eyes. "Alone."

"Forget it, boss."

Ben punched Wolf's arm, but the big man didn't let go. "I have to find her."

Oh, Ben. Kayla ached for him. For the pain he must be feeling at this moment. Part of her wanted to comfort him, to hold him in her arms and take away his pain. But that's not what he needed. He needed his daughter back.

Wolf hit Ben's jaw and he fell to the deck. Monk and Zach held him down. "Use your head, Ben."

He stopped struggling. A sense of purpose replaced the panicked expression on his face. "I'm okay."

The men continued to hold him against the deck.

"I won't jump." They released him and Ben stood. "Let's get the boats in the water. Move. Move."

As the crew went into action, Ben held out his hand to Kayla. "Come on."

Her heart filled with love and respect for the man in front of her. Before she could explain, she heard the curses from the other men. The yelling, the accusations, the fear. One boat wouldn't start. The other couldn't be launched. Total chaos.

"I don't have time for this, Kayla. Give me your hand."

Kayla knew what she had to do. Forget about Ben. Forget about fitting in. Forget about keeping her secret. Madison was the only thing that mattered.

"I'll bring her back to you." Kayla stared into his eyes. "Trust me, Ben."

She blew him a kiss and jumped into the water.

Trust her?

She'd just added to his problems. Damn, she wasn't wearing a life jacket. Ben didn't know if she could swim or not. He looked down at the water but didn't see Kayla come up. She had to be nearby. She needed air. A terrifying realization washed over him. He didn't want to lose her, too.

No, he was not going to lose either one of them. Not Madison. Not Kayla. "Kayla's overboard!"

He waited for her to surface. With each passing second, his level of anxiety increased tenfold. His pulse raced faster than a full-blown gale. He fought a battle of restraint, a war to hang on to his fragile control. "Does anyone see Madison or Kayla?"

The tension aboard multiplied. The shouting, cursing, activity increased.

"Dammit, I don't see them."

"The Little Bit's life jacket is missing."

"Do you see her?"

"Where's Kayla? I can't see Kayla."

Fear gushed down Ben's spine. He'd been afraid before, but never like this.

What was taking Kayla so damn long to surface? And what the hell was she thinking?

Jumping into the ocean wasn't like her. She wasn't

rash or a daredevil or irresponsible. She was smart enough to know how deadly and unforgiving the sea could be. He hoped Madison hadn't learned that yet.

Madison.

Ben stared at the water. His baby was out there. Alone, cold…breathing? The thought tore at his insides. His stomach constricted. Keep it together. His baby needed him.

"Madison!" He yelled until his voice gave out. He didn't care. He needed to do something, anything.

A scrap of white lace floated to the surface. Next came an orange jumpsuit. Kayla's. He stared at the clothing until it disappeared under a swell. Gone.

Kayla couldn't be gone, too.

Ben ignored the vise tightening around his heart. *Don't lose it.* Not with Madison still out there.

The sound of an engine roaring to life was the glimmer of hope he needed. But a part of him wished Kayla could have been it.

Kayla's tail appeared immediately. No pain, no discomfort.

The dolphin nudged her. He wanted Kayla to hurry.

She had to stop holding her breath, but learning to breathe underwater was scary and took getting used to. Everything else was okay. Maybe *okay* wasn't the proper word, but it would do for now.

Until she found Madison and returned her to Ben.

She struggled to keep up with the dolphin. Her tail propelled her through the water, but she wished she could go faster.

The longer she was in the water, the better her body adapted to being in the sea. It wasn't as cold as she'd thought it would be. The salt in the water no longer stung her eyes. She could see remarkably well.

The dolphin slowed. Kayla heard more dolphin noises—clicks of some sort. And then she saw an entire school of dolphins. In the center of them, two little feet attached to very human legs kicked as hard as they could. A glimpse of pink appeared—a pink life jacket.

Madison.

Kayla had never been more relieved in her entire life. She surfaced. "How are you doing, princess?"

"O-okay." Madison's face was pale, her lips bluish. "Look at all th-the dolphins, Kayla. They're my n-n-new friends. And I don't even have a t-tail."

"Are you hurt?"

Her teeth chattered. "I'm c-c-cold."

"I need to get you out of this water."

Madison nodded. "Are you a m-mermaid again?"

"Yes."

Kayla hugged the little girl's small, shivering body. Madison's eyelids looked heavy. Her eyes no longer sparkled. She rested her head against Kayla.

"I love you, Kayla."

A warmth surrounded Kayla's heart. She'd never felt anything like it before. Family. Her family. "I love you, too, Madison."

The seconds felt like minutes, the minutes like hours. It had taken Ben thirty seconds to realize he was getting in the way. He'd backed off and let his crew do the jobs they were trained to do. Distress calls had been sent, the boats were in the water and supplies readied—first-aid kits and stacks of towels and blankets.

All he could do was scan the water with binoculars

and pray. It wasn't much, but he had to do something or he would lose his mind.

Wolf stood next to him but didn't say a word. He surveyed the horizon with a pair of binoculars.

Ben concentrated on the water. Sunlight gleamed and looked like rivulets of mercury let loose over the swells. A deceptive beauty. That's what the sea was. He searched for a pair of heads bobbing up and down in the waves, but saw none.

The longer it took, the harder it got. That feeling in his stomach was getting worse. He'd survived tough, grim, nightmarish assignments in the navy, but nothing had prepared him for this.

Hold it together, Mendoza.

He wanted Kayla to find Madison. However unlikely. However improbable. He wanted to believe. He had to believe. A prayer, a wish, a dream. Whatever it would take, he wanted both of his girls back.

A breeze blew. The familiar scent of Wolf's aftershave drifted over and gave the moment a strange feeling of normalcy. Whether at sea or at land, it was as constant as his best friend's smile. And as powerful as his left hook. Ben sighed. "About earlier—"

"No need," Wolf interrupted. "I thought about jumping in myself."

Ben's eyes watered. He blinked. Hard. "Damn sun."

"It's a bright bugger today. Been bothering me, too," Wolf returned to surveying the water. "I don't believe it. She did it, Ben. Kayla's got Madison." Wolf laughed. "Hey, check out the dolphins swimming with them. Bet Madison is loving that."

Emotion clogged Ben's throat. His heart pounded with the force of a tsunami. His pulse raced faster than a hydroplane. Ben wasn't going to relax until both of them were aboard.

He stared in disbelief. The school of dolphins didn't take him by surprise. It was Kayla. She swam through the water with little effort. An Olympic gold medalist would have trouble with the heavy swells. It didn't make sense.

For once he didn't care. She had asked for his trust. An impossible request, but she hadn't let him down. If this was a dream come true, maybe he had to give dreams a chance.

Ben ran and met them at the stern of the ship. He scooped a wet and shivering Madison into his arms. He held her close, not wanting to let go of her. Ever.

His relief was overwhelming. It was almost as if he'd been holding his breath until this moment. "My princess."

Wolf wrapped three blankets around them. The big man's eyes were red-rimmed and he didn't want to let go of Madison's hand. Ben knew exactly how he felt.

"What happened, princess?" he asked.

Her face was pale. Her blue lips trembled. "I fell in."

He pulled her closer, hoping his body would warm her faster. "Why were you on the deck alone?"

Madison snuggled against him. "Baby Fifi was with me."

Monk handed over the doll. "She's right here, darlin'."

"Baby Fifi." Madison cried. "We wanted to have tails like Kayla." Madison sniffled. "But I don't have a tail."

Ben kissed her cheek and tasted saltwater. "Honey, Kayla doesn't have a tail."

"Yes, she does," Madison said. "Kayla's a mermaid, Daddy."

"Kayla's not—"

"Uh, boss," Wolf said. "I—I—I think she is. A m-mermaid."

What was going on? Ben turned to get reinforcement from Kayla, who sat on the deck. "Will you tell her…"

The words died on his lips. If it wasn't the sight of her bare breasts covered with her wet hair and the talisman hanging between them rendering him speechless, the green-and-blue tail would have done it.

"It's true." The edges of her mouth curved up. "I'm a mermaid, Ben."

"I told you, Daddy."

No, this wasn't happening. Mermaids didn't exist. Ben stared at Kayla, at her…tail. It defied every law of nature. "Who…what the hell are you?"

She winced. "As far as I know, I'm Kayla Waterton."

He wanted to look away, but he couldn't.

"Ben…" She said his name softly, and he shuddered. "I'm so sorry. I didn't want you to find out this way, but—"

"You aren't Kayla." Fear clawed its way into his heart. This wasn't the woman he'd kissed, the woman he'd fallen for, the woman he… "You aren't real."

"It's me." Kayla's eyes pleaded with him. "And I am real."

"No, you're not."

Ben had to get away; he had to get Madison away. Cradling her in his arms, he stood. Then he turned and ran.

Kayla sat, too stunned to cry. Her heart refused to believe what had just happened. She'd known the risk of jumping into the water, of showing her tail, but she thought—no, she truly believed Ben would understand and accept it.

Accept her.

Yes, it was unbelievable information to absorb, but the least he could have done was tried. Ben hadn't. She'd expected him to be baffled, confused, blown away. But she hadn't expected him to be afraid.

Just thinking about it again shattered her. Kayla choked back a cry and fought hard against the tears.

He didn't believe she was real.

A part of her wanted to give Ben the benefit of the doubt. Her entire life people had always said she was different—now she really was, and Kayla had questions about who and what she was, too. If the tail were on the other foot...

Who was she kidding? Kayla wouldn't care whether Ben was mer or Martian. The knowledge wouldn't change how she felt about him. It wouldn't change her love for him.

She loved him.

She loved Ben for who he was inside, not what he was outside. But he didn't feel the same about her. He most likely never had because he only saw what he wanted to see—Kayla the maritime historian.

Not Kayla the dreamer.

Definitely not Kayla the mermaid.

That realization hurt the most, but gave clarity to the situation. This wasn't about her. About her disappointing him. About her keeping a secret from him.

This was about Ben's fear and aversion to anything he didn't understand—dreams and mermaids and probably a lot of other things she didn't know about.

She shivered. Cold, tired, hurting.

Someone wrapped a blanket around her shoulders. Ben? She glanced up. It was Wolf.

Concern filled his eyes. "Do you need anything?"

"No, thanks, my legs will be back in about thirty minutes."

"So it's real?"

She didn't hear any fear or disgust. Only awe. "It's real."

"I've been at sea for almost twenty years and I never thought I'd ever see a mermaid." He smiled. "Pretty cool."

She appreciated his open-mindedness. "Thanks."

Monk joined them. "Can I touch your tail?"

Wolf elbowed him. "If the boss finds out you've touched anything…"

"Never mind, Kayla." Monk took a step back. "I'm addicted to breathing."

Wolf handed her towels. "Let's get you dried off."

Eugene gave her a water bottle; Stevie brought her a chocolate-chip cookie. The crew still accepted her, and that gave her hope.

"Does it hurt?" Fitz asked.

Her heart hurt and had shattered into a million pieces. But she knew he wasn't talking about her broken heart. "It hurt the first time I got the tail, but now it just feels a little weird. The strangest thing is being able to breathe underwater. That's going to take some getting used to."

"A real mermaid," Gray said.

"A real mermaid," she repeated.

She would rather be a real woman. A woman Ben could love. Not some half-fish, half-woman…creature.

But she was who she was. Nothing could change that. She couldn't change the past, nor could she change Ben.

He would either figure it out or he wouldn't. It was out of her hands.

Her love for Ben was strong enough to overcome this. She knew that in her heart. She only wondered about his.

Chapter Eleven

Sitting on the deck covered with a blanket, Kayla put on a T-shirt and waited for her legs to return so she could dress.

"Pappy's approaching on the starboard," Eugene said.

Kayla remembered the captain who had brought her to the *Xmarks Explorer*. To Ben. So much had changed since then.

Wolf shielded his eyes against the sun. "Delivering supplies?"

"People with cameras." Eugene's voice wavered.

Kayla's heart leapt. She clutched the blanket.

Wolf turned to Monk. "Go get Ben."

"No." Kayla wasn't ready to face him again. Not now, maybe not ever. "Madison needs him."

Wolf frowned. "Kayla, if they see you—"

"I'll spend the rest of my life in some laboratory or in a zoo. I know. I saw *Splash,* too." Kayla took a deep breath. It didn't help, but she had to remain calm. "It takes thirty minutes. I need more time."

Wolf moved a metal barrel in front of her. "You got it."

Kayla ducked. A minute later, she heard voices. A few she recognized. Several she didn't. The trickling of fear making its way down her back turned into Niagara Falls. Getting into the water was her safest option. She inched toward the rail.

"What the hell is going on?"

Kayla froze. She knew that voice. She peeked around the barrel. Ben stood with his hands on his hips, glaring at Pappy's passengers. A pirate never looked so dangerous. "I'm Ben Mendoza and this is my ship. Who are you?"

"I'm Phoebe Cartwright." A lovely woman with hair the color of honey and beautiful green eyes boarded the ship. Something about her seemed familiar, but Kayla didn't think they'd met before. "The captain mentioned something about a little girl falling overboard. I'm a doctor."

"My three-year-old daughter, Madison."

"Would you like me to take a look at her?"

"Please." Ben's relief reached all the way to Kayla. "Wolf, take Dr. Cartwright to Madison's cabin. I'll be right there."

As the doctor followed Wolf, a handsome man pushed his way past two other men. "Colin Bennett from All News Channel." Not a strand of his sandy blond hair was out of place. He smiled, his white teeth a stark contrast to his perfect tan. "We want to be the first to broadcast your news to the world."

Kayla's heart dropped to her feet—make that tail.

"News?" Ben glanced around. "We don't have any news."

His composure and nonchalant tone surprised Kayla. He'd reined in the emotion he'd shown earlier. He was totally in control of the situation and himself. Each crew member agreed they had no news, and tears filled her eyes.

"I don't understand." Colin frowned. "The Museum of Maritime History issued a press release about the discovery of the *Isabella*."

"Oh, the *Izzy*." Ben's smile reached his eyes. "We found her two days ago. I thought you meant new news."

Colin laughed. "Old news already, huh?"

"You have no idea." Ben motioned to Eugene. "Give Colin a tour of the ship, see where his crew wants to film and have Vance update him on our findings."

Kayla didn't know whether to be impressed or worried by Ben's professionalism. She glanced down. Her tail was gone. She slipped on the jumpsuit, wiped her eyes and combed her fingers through her tangled, damp hair. She couldn't stand it any longer. She wanted—needed—to be near Ben and talk with him. Explain things. At least try.

As Kayla made her way toward Ben, two more men boarded.

"Camera crew?" Ben asked them.

"No." A man with light-brown hair and blue eyes smiled. "I'm Kevin Cartwright, the doctor's husband."

"I'm Loucan." The second man's dark-brown hair was swept back from his high forehead and braided. "Friend of the family."

Nothing about him looked friendly. A shiver ran down

Kayla's spine. Loucan was so intimidating he made Ben look like a Cub Scout.

"Ben," Kayla said.

Everyone looked at her, everyone except Ben. He didn't glance her way, didn't acknowledge her at all. Tears stung her eyes, but she blinked them away. So this was how it would be.

Loucan stepped toward her. "Kai."

"This is Kayla Waterton." Ben stared past her as if she were invisible. The indifference on his face ripped at her heart. At least he'd said her name. "She's with the Museum of Maritime History in Portland, Oregon."

Loucan and Kevin exchanged a glance.

"Leave us," Loucan ordered. Everyone except Ben and Wolf left the deck. "Where did you get your necklace?"

"You don't need to answer their questions, Kayla." Ben sounded angry.

She appreciated his coming to her defense, but he still hadn't looked at her.

Kayla clutched her talisman for strength. "My father. Why?"

"Ianu," Kevin said to Loucan, who nodded.

Ben narrowed his gaze. "What the hell are you doing on my ship? You had no idea we'd need a doctor when you asked Pappy to bring you out here. What do you want?"

Loucan took another step toward her. He looked like a dangerous opponent, the kind of man you wanted on your team. "We read about the discovery of the *Isabella* and saw a picture of Kayla on the museum's Web site. Kevin is a private detective and he's been searching for Kai—Kayla."

"Me?" she asked.

Ben clenched his jaw. "Who wants to find her?"

"I do." Loucan touched her damp hair and tenderness filled his deep-blue eyes. "You've made the transformation."

Transformation.

Her dad had used the same word in his Atlantis stories, but it couldn't be possible....

Wolf moved between her and Loucan. "Get your hands off—"

"No, Wolf." Kayla didn't know Loucan or where he came from, but he knew she'd made the transformation. "Wh-who are you?"

"I'm Loucan." The edges of his mouth turned up, softening the hard lines of his face. "You are Kai. We are the same."

"We...?" Kayla forced the words out. "The same...?"

He breathed his reply, not even a whisper or a murmur, but she knew what he'd said.

Mer.

Loucan was mer.

Just like her.

Ben couldn't think straight. So much was happening. Interviews with the news crew. Kayla disappearing into her cabin with Loucan and Kevin. The doctor examining Madison. The only good news had been the doctor's diagnosis.

Madison was fine.

He stared at her, safe and sound in her bed. He'd come so close to losing her. Big changes were in store. Locks, gates, video-surveillance equipment. Nothing like this would happen again.

Madison stretched out her arms. "Daddy."

"How are you feeling, princess?"

"Good." She patted her bed. "Look at all my blankets. I got candy and hot chocolate. Uncle Stevie put whipped cream on it."

Ben smiled. "Sounds like tummyache time."

"I didn't eat all of it. I saved some for my new friends."

Ben sat on the edge of the bed. "What new friends?"

"My dolphin friends. I really like them. They like me, too. Can I have them over to play?"

"That might be difficult, princess." He stroked her hair. "Dolphins live in the water. It wouldn't be good for them to come aboard the ship."

"Oh." She drew her lower lip between her teeth. "Then only Kayla can play with them." As quickly as the pout started, it disappeared. "Did you see us swim, Daddy? We went so fast. Kayla told me to hold on tight and I did."

"You sure did." And for that Ben was grateful. He owed a great deal to Kayla, but he couldn't even look at her.

"Kayla can live in the water *and* on the ship." Madison smiled. "Where is she now? Can she play with me?"

Her question squeezed his already aching heart. "Kayla is busy, honey. She's…getting ready to leave." He hoped. He wanted her gone. Wolf called him a chicken. Ben didn't care.

"Where's she going? When's she coming back?"

Never. "I don't know," he admitted. "Madison, Kayla's… Well, she's…different."

"She's not different." Madison beamed. "She's Kayla."

"Princess—"

"Ask her to live with us, Daddy? Please, oh, please, oh, please." Her brown eyes implored him and his heart sank. This was one thing he couldn't do for his daughter. "I don't want Kayla to leave. I love her. Don't you love her, Daddy?"

"Do you love him?" Dr. Phoebe Cartwright asked.

Kayla sat on the bed next to her. "Love who?"

"Whatever man has you so torn up inside."

She couldn't imagine her feelings, her heartbreak, being so transparent. But Phoebe wasn't just any stranger. Kayla had just discovered Phoebe was her twin sister. "I've been through a lot today. That's all."

Madison's rescue had been only the beginning of a surreal afternoon. Kayla had learned more answers about her past. Answers nothing could have prepared her to hear.

She connected her talisman to the one Phoebe wore. The two pieces fit perfectly together and formed a half circle, but the other half was missing. According to Phoebe, those two pieces belonged to their brother, Saeger, and sister, Thalassa. Phoebe's husband, Kevin, was a private detective hired by Loucan to find all of the siblings and their talismans. He needed the completed seal to unlock the treasures of the underwater kingdom where she had been born. Pacifica, not Atlantis. The name was different, but the story the same.

Phoebe touched the top of her hand. "Kai—"

"My name's Kayla."

"I'm sorry." Phoebe's tone was genuine. "Ever since I learned I had a twin sister, I've thought of you as Kai."

"I'll get used to it, but life as I know it has changed. I'd like to hang on to something that was me. The old me."

"I understand." And Phoebe did. She'd been as surprised when she learned about her past from Loucan. "I know what you've been through today and what you've learned about yourself."

Kayla rubbed her fingertip over the talismans. Her name wasn't Kayla, but Kai. Jason Waterton, known among the mer as Ianu, was not her father, but a mer guardian appointed by her biological father, King Okeana, to keep Kayla safe during a bitter civil war. Her mother, Queen Wailele, hadn't drowned, but was killed during a battle between the breathers and the swimmers. Her family was swimmers; Loucan's, breathers. But those differences were in the past.

"But there's more," Phoebe said. "You've been hurt. It's in your eyes, and I'm guessing in your heart, too."

Kayla's gaze sought Phoebe's. "How did you know?"

"Been there, done that with Kevin."

"But the two of you are so perfect together."

"Thanks." Phoebe smiled. "But you should have seen us when Kevin first found me. We were far from perfect together."

Kayla sighed. So were she and Ben. And always would be. Her heart ached. Someday the pain would heal. Someday soon, she hoped.

"That bad?" Phoebe asked.

Kayla's cheeks warmed. This was her twin sister, she reminded herself. "Ben and I were together, but it didn't…"

"What happened?"

"I never told him I was a mermaid. When I brought Madison back to the ship…" Kayla had gained one family but lost another. Ben and Madison. The crew. Emotion clogged Kayla's throat. "When he saw me…the look in his eyes, the fear."

"He needs time. It's not every day you see a mermaid."

Kayla separated the two talismans. "I can't wait for Ben to come around." Her heart told her he was the one, but only if he accepted her. "Loucan offered to escort me to Pacifica. He said I would be safe from Joran there."

Joran was a mer who wanted the four necklaces so he could steal the treasure for himself. He was dangerous and would stop at nothing to achieve his goal.

"No one has seen Joran in months. He could be dead." Phoebe's eyes clouded. "You can come with Kevin and me."

"Thanks, but you're newlyweds—"

"You're my sister." Phoebe took her hand. "Family."

Family. The word encompassed so much. So many. Tears welled in Kayla's eyes. Jason or Ianu. He would always be her father—the one who had raised her, loved her, protected her. Loucan had explained her father's obsession with the *Isabella.* Ianu located shipwrecks for Pacifica. The last ship he'd found before taking Kayla away and shedding his tail and gills to keep their past a secret had been the *Isabella.* He'd never completed the work he'd started as a mer so the location remained a mystery to the residents of Pacifica.

"It's still so hard to believe." Kayla sighed. "It seems like a dream."

Phoebe gave her hand a gentle squeeze. "I know."

"And I know what I want to do. I want to see Pacifica." Kayla handed Phoebe her necklace. "But first I have to talk with Ben. Say…goodbye."

"I'll be here if you need me."

"Thanks."

Phoebe hugged her. "That's what sisters are for."

Ben watched Kevin Cartwright work on the computer in the communications room. Things kept getting more complicated by the minute, and he didn't know what to do. He'd learned the true identities of Phoebe and Lou-can.

Kayla was with two others like herself. Ben tried to tell himself that having them here was a good thing. "So you trust old fish boy?"

Kevin looked away from the computer monitor. "Who?"

"Loucan."

"It's not so much a matter of trust. He hired me to find Phoebe and her siblings. I'm just doing my job." Kevin typed on the keyboard. "What about you?"

"Me?"

"Are you going to let him swim off with your woman?"

"She's not my woman." At Kevin's pointed glance, Ben leaned against the desk. "She's a mermaid."

"So is Phoebe. Let me tell you, she has one nice tail."

He couldn't believe how normal Kevin sounded talking about his wife. Merwife? Ben didn't want to go there. "Loucan seems dangerous. He's always lurking around."

"He shows up when you least expect it, but the guy's good stuff. He needs to find all four talismans."

Ben shrugged. "I've been wondering what my cook could do with him. Loucan Thermidor. Grill him with a white wine sauce."

"Don't forget the capers and garlic."

"And a twist of lemon."

Kevin smiled. "Thanks for letting me use your computer. I'd better see what Phoebe is up to."

As soon as Kevin left, Ben called his parents. On the third ring, his father answered.

"Hey, Dad. Is Mom home?"

"No, she's having her hair done."

Silence. The miles separating them seemed to increase.

His dad cleared his throat. "Congrats on discovering the *Isabella,* son. I always knew you'd find her."

The pride in his father's voice brought a lump to Ben's throat. He'd succeeded. Not with dreams, but with hard work. "Thanks."

"So what's up next?"

"We'll bring up the artifacts and—"

"No," his dad interrupted. "I meant what ship are you going after once you're done with the *Isabella?*"

"There's more gold than you can imagine." At least that was one good piece of information Loucan had relayed. "I won't have to go after another ship. Ever."

"What will you do?"

"Don't know, but I won't have to worry about money."

"Dreams are more valuable than any treasure, son."

"How can you say that?" Ben gripped the receiver. "You always talk about hitting the big one. Finding the mother lode."

"True, but given the choice I'd rather have my dreams. That's what matters, not whether you hit the jackpot or not."

His father sounded just like Kayla.

Kayla.

A heaviness centered in Ben's chest. "Dad, this is a strange question, but do you believe in mermaids?"

"I never really thought about it before, but it would be a shame not to believe."

"It would be unreal."

His father sighed. "Could you imagine anything more wonderful than an honest-to-goodness mermaid?"

Ben could think of several. "Thanks, Dad."

''Keep sending those e-mails and give Madison a kiss. Love you, son.''

Ben hung up the phone and laughed. His father, the ultimate dreamer, thought seeing a mermaid would be wonderful.

Wonderful? It was anything but wonderful. Unbelievable, out-of-this-world, wacky.

Wacky Waterton.

That's what Kayla's classmates had called her. None of them had ever looked further than the name. Ben's heart sank. He wasn't looking further than her tail.

Damn. He was as guilty as all of them. No, it was worse. He knew her, cared for her.

Loved her.

And he'd hurt her. Walked away from her when she needed him most.

What an idiot he'd been. Kayla had given him everything. She'd located the *Izzy.* Saved his daughter. Given him her heart.

Never once had he given her anything in return. All she wanted him to do was to dream, to believe. He'd failed in the worst possible way. Failed her. Failed himself.

So Kayla was a mermaid? If that was the worst thing they had to deal with, they would be lucky.

Ben only wondered if it was too late for a ''they.''

Kayla had told him it was never too late to dream. He hoped she was right.

Chapter Twelve

Standing at the railing, Kayla gazed at the vast amount of water stretching beyond the horizon. This was her new world. She just wasn't ready to leave her old world yet.

"Mind if I join you?" Ben asked.

She gripped the railing so hard her knuckles turned white. "Please do. Join me, that is."

Rays from the setting sun gleamed in his black hair. "How are you doing?"

Her life had been inverted and submerged underwater. His reaction hadn't helped matters, but he was talking to her. That was a positive sign. "Okay, I guess."

"A lot of info to chew on, huh?"

"You could say that." Talking like this as if nothing had happened felt strange. But it was easier and safer. She needed a little of both right now.

Dolphins frolicked in the distance, their chatter a soothing melody. The smell of the sea tickled her nose, but the salt was also a comforting scent.

"Kayla."

"Ben," she said at the same time. "You go first."
After goodbye, Kayla didn't know what else could be
said.

"Thanks." Ben took a deep breath. "I'm sorry I
freaked out this afternoon. But when I saw you and your
tail…it was so unbelievable, so unreal. Mermaids were
something Madison dreamed about. They weren't real. I
wasn't ready to face the truth."

"And now?"

He looked down at her legs. "I'm getting there."

A start. Kayla released the breath she'd been holding.

"I prided myself on being practical and realistic.
Dreams were a waste of time. Worthless. Not real. Seeing you proved me wrong. I was too proud to admit it
earlier, but now… Dreams and mermaids." A trace of
wonder filled his voice. "Who am I to say what's real
or not?"

"They're real if you believe." She wanted to hold on
to the glimmer of hope she saw. "The magic is in the
dream."

Ben nodded. "My father said something similar. I
spoke with him tonight."

Kayla knew how Ben felt about his dad. She touched
his shoulder. When she realized what she had done, she
pulled her hand away. "How did it go?"

"Better than I imagined it would." Ben sighed. "Tonight I realized he's happy just chasing his dreams.
That's more important than making them come true."

"Did you tell your father?"

"No. Not yet." Ben's jaw tensed. "All my life, I've
wanted to succeed. To be the exact opposite of my father. I found the *Izzy*. My father never fulfilled one of

his dreams. But I'm not happy and he is. I need to re-think my definition of success and failure.''

''It's not that simple.''

''I know.'' A wry grin graced his lips. ''You showed me dreams aren't black-and-white. Neither is life. If I hadn't been so closed-minded, so practical, I could have shared my father's dreams. We could have found the *Izzy* together.''

''It's not too late.''

He touched her arm. ''I hope not.''

The small gesture meant so much. Kayla wished she could ignore the tingles racing up her arm.

''I was so worried about the cost of dreaming, I didn't see the price I was paying for not dreaming. For not believing. I want to believe, Kayla. In everything. In us.''

She swallowed. Hard. ''Us?''

''Us.'' His gaze locked with hers. ''Words can never make up for the way I treated you, but I'm sorry. I hope you'll let me make it up to you.''

The sincere look in his eyes filled her with warmth. She knew he meant each and every word. ''Apology accepted.''

''You forgive me?''

''I do.'' Kayla smiled. ''I'm sorry I didn't tell you I was a mermaid, but I only found out about it the day before we found the *Isabella*. At first I thought I was allergic to something because of the itching. And then I thought it was because I was falling for you.''

''For me?''

She nodded. ''Pounding heart, rapid pulse, sweaty palms, butterflies in my stomach.''

He laced his fingers with hers and she drew strength from his touch. ''Kayla...''

"When I discovered the truth about being a mermaid, I was afraid of losing you. Nothing like finding out you're half fish to make you start doubting yourself. And everything else."

"Kayla, if I'd known…" She raised a brow and he grinned. "Okay, I still would have freaked out, but I'm sorry you had to go through that alone."

She knew what he'd meant. Her heart pounded so loudly she couldn't hear anything else. She had to say this. She might not get another chance. "I came on this expedition because I wanted answers. I thought I needed them to go forward with my life. But I found something more important. Two things, actually. You and Madison."

"I know how you feel about Madison." He squeezed her hand. "You saved her life. I can never repay you enough for that."

"You don't have to repay me." Kayla took a deep breath. "I love you, Ben."

His eyes widened.

She smiled. "You can be bold and daring, sweet and tender, practical and pigheaded. You're more pirate than prince. But those things make you who you are—the man I love."

"Kayla…"

She placed her fingertips on his lips. "You don't have to say anything."

"I want to say something."

His gaze was practically a caress. She recognized the tenderness in his eyes. It was the same the first time he'd kissed her. A lump formed in her throat.

"I love you, too." Ben's words and his smile took her breath away. "I didn't want to, I tried hard not to, but somehow it happened. You're not only a mermaid, but a siren sent here to humble me, to make me a better father and a better man."

The depth of emotion overwhelmed her. Tears stung her eyes.

He pushed a strand of hair off her face. "You're gorgeous, smart, funny and you made me want to believe that dreams do come true. The only thing wrong is…"

Her heart skipped a beat. "What?"

"Madison wishes your tail could be pink." He smiled. "She likes how it sparkles, so I'm sure she'll get used to it being blue and green and silver."

It was almost too much to hope for. "Almost" being the operative word. "You want me to stay?"

"Damn straight, I want you to stay."

"Oh, Ben." A warm glow settled around her heart. "There's so much I learned today. So much I need to tell you."

"You're the woman I love." He stared into her eyes. "That's all I need to know."

"But I'm also a mermaid. If people find out—"

He kissed her, his lips warm and firm against hers. "It will be okay. Whatever happens, we'll figure it out. Together. You, me and Madison." Ben smiled. "Let us be part of your world, Kayla."

"Kai." The voice came from the bow. As Loucan walked down the staircase, his steps echoed. He reached the bottom and stared at her. His brow furrowed. "We must leave immediately."

She was home. She didn't have to go anywhere else. A satisfied smile formed. "I'm staying here."

Ben wrapped his arm around her shoulder. "With me."

Loucan's lips narrowed. "You and he—"

"My name's Ben," he said. "And Kayla and I are getting married."

Married. Okay, he hadn't got down on his knee and proposed romantically, but she had no complaints. Kayla was marrying a pirate, not a poet. Joy flowed through her. "We're getting married."

Loucan glared at Ben. "She could be in danger from Joran."

"I'll keep her safe."

She would be safe with Ben. Safe, secure and happy. The *Isabella* had kept Luis and Ana apart, but it had brought Kayla and Ben together. "I'll be fine."

The two men stared at each other.

"We would like you to attend the wedding," Ben said.

"Thank you." Loucan sounded anything but pleased.

Kayla thought he looked disappointed. She wanted everyone to be as happy as she was. "Please know I'll do whatever I can to help you. I want to find my brother and sister, too."

Loucan's gaze held hers. "Thank you, Kai."

She smiled. "I'd really like to see Pacifica one day."

"Me, too," Ben said.

Loucan nodded to both of them before leaving them alone.

Ben pulled her closer. "What if we go to Pacifica for our honeymoon?"

She loved the idea, except the logistics boggled her mind. "How will you…?"

A smug smile formed. "The submersible."

"Still, once we're there…"

"Don't forget, hon, I was a navy diver." Pride laced each one of his words. "I know how to swim."

He brushed his lips over hers, and Kayla's heart sang with delight. "Do you think you can keep up with me?"

His warm breath tickled her neck. "I'll happily spend the rest of my life trying."

* * * * *

*Don't miss the third enchanting title in
the Silhouette Romance miniseries,*
A TALE OF THE SEA,
with the September 2002 release of
CAUGHT BY SURPRISE (SR1614)

SILHOUETTE Romance™

**Lost siblings, secret worlds,
tender seduction—live the fantasy in...**

A TALE OF THE SEA

**Separated and hidden since childhood,
Phoebe, Kai, Saegar and Thalassa
must reunite in order to safeguard
their underwater kingdom.
But who will protect *them*...?**

July 2002
MORE THAN MEETS THE EYE
by Carla Cassidy (SR #1602)

August 2002
IN DEEP WATERS
by Melissa McClone (SR #1608)

September 2002
CAUGHT BY SURPRISE
by Sandra Paul (SR #1614)

October 2002
FOR THE TAKING
by Lilian Darcy (SR #1620)

*Look for these titles wherever
Silhouette books are sold!*

Where love comes alive™

Visit Silhouette at www.eHarlequin.com   SRTOS

Silhouette

SPECIAL EDITION™

&

SILHOUETTE *Romance*®

present a new series about the proud,
passion-driven dynasty

THE
COLTONS

**You loved the California Coltons, now discover
the Coltons of Black Arrow, Oklahoma.
Comanche blood courses through their veins,
but a brand-new birthright awaits them....**

WHITE DOVE'S PROMISE by Stella Bagwell (7/02, SE#1478)

THE COYOTE'S CRY by Jackie Merritt (8/02, SE#1484)

WILLOW IN BLOOM by Victoria Pade (9/02, SE#1490)

THE RAVEN'S ASSIGNMENT by Kasey Michaels (9/02, SR#1613)

A COLTON FAMILY CHRISTMAS by Judy Christenberry,
Linda Turner and Carolyn Zane (10/02, Silhouette Single Title)

SKY FULL OF PROMISE by Teresa Southwick (11/02, SR#1624)

THE WOLF'S SURRENDER by Sandra Steffen (12/02, SR#1630)

*Look for these titles
wherever Silhouette books are sold!*

Silhouette®

Where love comes alive™

Visit Silhouette at www.eHarlequin.com   SSECOLT

**Where royalty and romance
go hand in hand...**

The series continues in Silhouette Romance
with these unforgettable novels:

HER ROYAL HUSBAND
by Cara Colter
on sale July 2002 (SR #1600)

THE PRINCESS HAS AMNESIA!
by Patricia Thayer
on sale August 2002 (SR #1606)

SEARCHING FOR HER PRINCE
by Karen Rose Smith
on sale September 2002 (SR #1612)

And look for more Crown and Glory stories in
SILHOUETTE DESIRE starting in October 2002!

Available at your favorite retail outlet.

Where love comes alive™

Visit Silhouette at www.eHarlequin.com   SRCAG

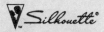

SPECIAL EDITION™

Was it something in the water...
or something in the air?

Because bachelors in Bridgewater, Texas,
are becoming a vanishing breed—fast!

**Don't miss these three exciting stories of Texas
cowboys by favorite author Jodi O'Donnell:**

Deke Larrabie returns to discover
someone *else* he left behind....

THE COME-BACK COWBOY
(Special Edition #1494)
September 2002

Connor Brody meets his match and gives her

THE RANCHER'S PROMISE
(Silhouette Romance #1619)
October 2002

Griff Corbin learns about true
friendship and love when he falls for

HIS BEST FRIEND'S BRIDE
(Silhouette Romance #1625)
November 2002

Available at your favorite retail outlet.

Where love comes alive™

Visit Silhouette at www.eHarlequin.com   SSEBRB

A powerful earthquake ravages Southern California...

Thousands are trapped beneath the rubble...

The men and women of Morgan Trayhern's team face their most heroic mission yet...

A brand-new series from *USA TODAY* bestselling author

LINDSAY McKENNA

Don't miss these breathtaking stories of the triumph of love!

Look for one title per month from each Silhouette series:

August: THE HEART BENEATH
(Silhouette Special Edition #1486)

September: RIDE THE THUNDER
(Silhouette Desire #1459)

October: THE WILL TO LOVE
(Silhouette Romance #1618)

November: PROTECTING HIS OWN
(Silhouette Intimate Moments #1185)

Available at your favorite retail outlet

Where love comes alive™

Visit Silhouette at www.eHarlequin.com   SXSMMUR

eHARLEQUIN.com

| | | | | community | membership |
| buy books | authors | online reads | magazine | learn to write |

Visit eHarlequin.com to discover your one-stop
shop for romance:

buy books

♥ Choose from an extensive selection of Harlequin,
Silhouette, MIRA and Steeple Hill books.

♥ Enjoy top Silhouette authors and *New York Times*
bestselling authors in Other Romances: Nora Roberts,
Jayne Ann Krentz, Danielle Steel and more!

♥ Check out our deal-of-the-week specially discounted
books at up to 30% off!

♥ Save in our Bargain Outlet: hard-to-find books at great
prices! Get 35% off your favorite books!

♥ Take advantage of our low-cost flat-rate shipping
on all the books you want.

♥ Learn how to get FREE Internet-exclusive books.

♥ In our Authors area find the currently available titles of
all the best writers.

♥ Get a sneak peek at the great reads for the next
three months.

♥ Post your personal book recommendation online!

♥ Keep up with all your favorite miniseries.

Silhouette®

where love comes alive™—online...

Visit us at
www.eHarlequin.com

SINTBB

MONTANA
MAVERICKS

One of Silhouette Special Edition's most popular series returns with three sensational stories filled with love, small-town gossip, reunited lovers, a little murder, hot nights and the best in romance:

HER MONTANA MAN
by Laurie Paige
(ISBN#: 0-373-24483-5)
Available August 2002

BIG SKY COWBOY
by Jennifer Mikels
(ISBN#: 0-373-24491-6)
Available September 2002

MONTANA LAWMAN
by Allison Leigh
(ISBN#: 0-373-24497-5)
Available October 2002

*True love is the only way to beat the heat
in Rumor, Montana....*

Silhouette®

Where love comes alive™

COMING NEXT MONTH